Bayou Shadows

Bayou Shadows

A NOVEL

B.J. Foster

FIRST EDITION

First Printing, March, 2000
10 9 8 7 6 5 4 3 2 1

Library of Congress Cataloging-in-Publication Data
ISBN: 0-9675884-5-6 (hardcover)

Printed in the United States of America

Cresent House Publishing
9333 Memorial Drive, Suite 215
Houston, Texas 77024
713-268-4763
cresenthouse@usa.net

For Leonard and Sharon, both whom had more confidence in me than I had in myself.

ACKNOWLEDGEMENTS

With heartfelt thanks to Barbara Reeves, my teacher who cracked the whip and my friend who encouraged. Also many thanks to my friends of the High Country Writers Group for their inspiration and special thanks to Maggie Bishop, Marian Coe, Virginia Abercrombie and Lila Hopkins. Lt. Mike Hayes, deputy sheriff St. Martin Parrish for his help and assistance.

Bayou Shadows

Chapter One

"Are you all right, Miss?" Strong arms reached out to steady her.

"Oooh yes, I'm sorry." Embarrassed, Stacy quickly stepped back and ran her hands over her dress smoothing wrinkles. "I'm afraid I was in a hurry and not looking where. . . ." She glanced up into a grinning devilishly handsome face. The words caught and froze in her throat. She'd hit what felt like a padded wall.

He released her shoulders, letting his hands slide down her arms. Dark eyes swallowed her. He wouldn't let her break eye contact and she felt her face flush. He was tall and hard muscled she'd discovered by the impact. Black wavy hair skimmed his collar. The top button of his crisp cream shirt was unfastened and the

1

silk foulard tie loosened. His tobacco brown suit set off his tan and Stacy was sure he knew it. She thought wrong place, wrong time. Maybe someday a good-looking man like you will come along but there's no room in my plans for anyone now.

He reached down to retrieve the scattered clippings. As he rose, he absorbed her presence starting with her high heels and working his way to her sparkling dark eyes. Placing the articles into her hands, a slanted smile crept across his face. His cool hand lingered over hers. Black eyes gleamed telling her he liked what he saw. "Have you considered trying out for defensive guard on the Saints?" He chuckled.

Stacy glanced around to see if eyes in the newsroom were watching them. "I'm so sorry," she repeated. Her mind had been on getting to Mitch McGalliard's office before other business of the day demanded the editor's attention.

"No damage done, but you'd better get in there. Your boss is making noise like a trumpeting bull elephant. He said to tell you he'd give you ten seconds then he's got another conference."

"Yes, yes, I'd better." Stacy was still shaken by the surprise encounter but refocused her attention on her mission. She hurried towards Mitch's door and disappeared.

The stranger watched her high heels click across the floor and smiled to himself. He had spied her earlier through the glass windows in Mitch's office and asked who she was. Her dark bouncing curls had first caught his attention but as his eyes drifted over her body, the swaying of her petite frame suggested something mysterious—not yet disillusioned with time but energized with what life offered and this excited him. He couldn't see her eyes, but he didn't need to. He knew they were the color of nutmeg and danced with her smile.

Mitch had beat around the bush in answering him saying she was just a kid from the swamp with a determined eye. Whatever that meant. Intrigued, he'd meant to introduce himself as he played messenger boy for Mitch but it all happened so fast. Even so, he patted himself on the back. Couldn't have timed that collision better he thought.

The garden and society page was burying Stacy along with gladiola bulbs and yesterdays grand-dames of New Orleans. She was never going to get where she wanted to be unless she captured more credibility and this story was one that could put her on the right track. Now she just had to convince Mitch that it was a dynamite story.

She found Mitch talking on the phone and jotting notes at the same time. He motioned her to sit down and completed his conversation. Placing the receiver in its cradle asked, "So whatcha you got?" He still

3

scribbled along on the pad not wasting any time.

Stacy took a deep breath and began, "Publicity chairman for the historical society called. Needs an article for the annual membership drive. I've been doing some research and found some clips on the Townsend plantation." She scattered the articles across his desk.

He took one glance and reared back in his chair. "I know a little something about that place." Without taking a breath he continued. "The story's been beat to death and it's up for auction soon."

That should have been the end of discussion but Stacy refused to let it go that easily. She fingered her way through the clippings on the desk and rested a manicured nail on one. "What about this angle?"

Mitch read the first line. *Oil Companies Gobbling Up Historical Lands.* His mouth gave a small twitch at the corner. The obstinate lock of sandy brown hair that always seemed to find its way into his blue-green eyes quivered. He made a swipe at it and glanced pointed back at her. "You think you can pull that off without landing us in a lawsuit?"

Stacy smiled, "Certainly like the opportunity to try."

"I think you're a gluten for punishment but see what you can do with it." Pointing his pen at her he added, "And Stacy, I need to know that it's not going to cause us any trouble. If it doesn't run, I don't want to hear any gnashing of teeth."

Stacy felt the leap of victory and hastily nodded. "Agreed."

"Know where it's located?"

"Yes, I know." Her heart pounded. She thought her teeth would melt with the boldface lie but knew she'd do the same thing again. She turned crisply on her heels and pulled the door closed behind her before he could change his mind.

Sweaty palms clung to the clippings leaving her hands inky black. How was she going to locate the Townsend Plantation? Second-guessing herself, she wished she'd admitted she didn't know where it was. Mitch would have told her. One thing was certain, she couldn't go back now. He'd know she'd lied.

Stacy had accepted the cub reporter job to be able to work for Mitch McGalliard. He'd earned the reputation of being one of the best editors in the South. His boyish good looks belied his experience. His eyes didn't look at you; they looked through you. Stacy felt he always knew the answer to the question before he asked it. If you lied, he'd know it before you got your mouth shut and she had just done that.

Stacy glanced around the newsroom and stopped at the mail clerks desk. "Ted, where is Boudreaux Lake? Mitch said it was somewhere in Terrebonne Parish."

Ted was a native. He knew every little road, pig trail, and bayou in Louisiana. Taking a map from a drawer, he placed a red dot in the left corner, folded and handed it to her.

"Thanks, I owe you," she said and headed for her car. Finally a real story. Maybe there wouldn't be anymore society drivel to cover. Don't mess up, she admonished herself.

Everything was going according to schedule until she came to an old narrow plank bridge across the swamp. One wheel off this and she was sure she'd spend eternity out here with the water moccasins. She sighed, "Easy does it."

Slowly the car rolled up onto the first board. Each plank rattled and snapped as the tires passed over it.

"Lord, let it be solid," she prayed and held her breath. No one had mentioned the rickety old bridges on these back roads. But she was here now; going back wasn't an option. She breathed a little easier when the car rolled over the last timber and onto terra firma.

Her mind sped back to her childhood of growing up in the Big Thicket. The undergrowth of the forest and the bogginess of the river bottom were much like this. She remembered the Saturdays she spent on Old River fishing by herself. Momma didn't like Stacy to be on the river alone in the little skiff but she knew Stacy did it anyway. Stacy liked hunting for worms under the old sheet of rusty corrugated tin in back of the barn. She liked to feel them squirm as she retrieved a fat one for her hook.

She knew water moccasins sunned themselves on low limbs hanging out over the river. She had to be careful where she put her hands. She also knew that she would make about two good mouthfuls for the 'gators looking like logs lying along the banks. Stacy loved being alone on the water and listening to the alive sounds of creatures in the river bottom: the sudden loud splash of the water as a big bass claimed the dragonfly lighting on the surface of the river, hawks screeching as they flew through the cypress tops. Most of all, she loved the independence she experienced—even at the age of ten.

The car sloshed into a deep mud hole, jolting her back to reality. Surely, it couldn't be much farther. She checked the map again. She wasn't sure how far she had driven. The road curved around a dense field of pines. Old oaks lined either side of the road. The trunks were huge and the limbs touched the earth and rebounded. They echoed the history of more than a century.

An old mansion came into view through branches of live oaks laden with Spanish moss. The paint had worn so thin that the old home appeared gray as a ghost. Shingles had blown from the roof and lay scattered about the yard. One of the shattered windows had been covered with boards. Even in such neglected condition, its beauty took her breath away. What a place it must have been in its day, she thought.

The car rolled to a stop in front of a scrolled wrought iron gate. She slammed the car door loudly enough for anyone in the house to hear and walked slowly toward the large pillared verandah.

Suddenly, three large hound dogs came at her on a dead run from the side of the house, their barking malicious, their teeth bared. Her heart skipped a beat and landed in her throat. She was already too far from the car to retreat. The dogs were almost on her when she spied a chink in their bluff. The oldest of the dogs, a spotted Catahoula hound with his tail wagging, caught the back of the neck of the lead dog riding him into the dirt in a playful prank. The others followed his lead and ceased their barking. Stacy hoped her nervousness didn't reveal itself in her voice. They would sense it immediately if she displayed fear and probably take advantage of it. "Well, hello there, fellas." She extended her small hand hoping not to pull back a nub.

The dogs sniffed at her hand and legs. When the older dog was satisfied that she posed no threat, he welcomed her gentle stroking. Now they all wanted to be petted. The smallest of the group flopped on the ground at her feet and turned his feet up in the air to receive the much-coveted attention. As she knelt to pet the smaller animal, the old spotted one licked the side of her mouth. Stacy laughed and wiped her mouth with the back of her hand.

"Here. Here." A thin weather beaten old man

shouted from the doorway and stepped onto the verandah. Hanging onto a banister for support, he descended the stairs as quickly as his fragile bones would take the steps. He hollered across the yard. "Those dogs don't generally let strangers even get out of the car. Seems they took to you right off. You've been around dogs, I bet."

"I love dogs," Stacy replied.

He patted his hand gently on the hound's back. "They always know if you're afraid of 'em. That's for sure."

Stacy continued to lavish attention on them for a few seconds and then stood to introduce herself.

"I'm Stacy Stimmons, from *The Times-Picayune.* I'm supposed to do a story on the Townsend Plantation."

"Yeah, some woman from the paper called about writing a story. They said somebody would be out."

"Yes, I called."

Josh continued as if he hadn't heard her. "Didn't say it would be a school girl though. Why'd they let you come all the way out here by yourself?"

Stacy smiled at the compliment. "I'm afraid those days are long past. Are you Mr. Townsend?"

He nodded. "I'm Josiah Townsend. Guess you'll want to look around."

"Yes, and I'd like to know some of the history of the plantation. I understand you're planning to auction the property soon. If you can show me the furnishings and a few of the items you want to include in the auction, I think it would add some interest for the readers."

"Well, it all goes," he said resolutely. "I'm just getting too old to give the place the care it needs. My nephew would like to see it stay in the family, but he doesn't have the money to keep it up." He gazed around the homestead with tired watery eyes; the love he held for the place revealed itself. How sad it must be to have to give up your home at this time of life. The moment hung with silence.

"Think I'm going down to Miami and get me one of those condo things. They tell me there's plenty of 'widder' women down there to invite me to dinner, too." The wiry, old man chuckled shallowly his eyes snapping with mischief. Stacy liked him instantly.

She detected weariness and sadness in his voice in spite of his attempt at lightness. "How long have you owned the plantation, Mr. Townsend?"

"My great granddad built this place just after the War Between the States. Wanted to get just as far from the stink of war as he could." He shook his head. "Brought a wife and three kids out here from Virginia. Saw this bottomland, knew it'd grow about anything. Settled on cotton, sugarcane, and rice."

Stacy could visualize crops swaying in the wind and the house gleaming white.

"Bought five hundred acres and kept addin' 'til

there was near four thousand acres. Had three boys that kept it up. My great granny Townsend named it Dawn's Promise because it was giving them a new beginning after the horrors of the war."

"How did you acquire it, Mr. Townsend?" Stacy scribbled as fast as she could, attempting to get every word.

"When William Ryan Townsend died, that was my granddad, it was divided equally among the three boys. The kids of my two great uncles just wasted money on fast living. They sold off most of their shares. My Dad, that was Richard Ryan, bought back what he could afford from them. My younger brother George, and I inherited from him."

He pointed a shaking finger at a small hill to the side of the house. "George was killed in World War II. He's buried up there on that high ground with my wife and kin." The old man took a long deep breath and continued. "Through the years, bits and pieces been sold off to keep the place going. Now there's nothing left except a thousand acres, the house, stables and some other out buildings. With taxes being what they are now, I can't hold on to it any longer," he added matter-of-factly.

"Get out of the way, Scooter." He kicked half-heartily at the dog lying in the walkway.

They had reached the verandah when an old Chevy pulled up in front.

11

"Here's my nephew. Went up to Virginia and made a lawyer. Real proud of that boy."

A tall man dressed in jeans, a yellow polo shirt with a navy blazer and loafers, got out and started toward them. The dogs ran to the gate but didn't bark, only wagged their tails and sniffed at his heels. Obviously he wasn't a stranger. A grin lit up his face as he recognized Stacy.

Stacy identified the dark disarming eyes and rakish smile immediately. It was the man she had collided with in the office. His dark, Ivy League styled hair was clean cut except for the escaping curl coiling over his collar. Ralph Lauren from top to bottom.

Bending down to rub the dog's ears he said, "Hey, Scooter, did you and Rascal get a rabbit today?" His voice was clear and kind as he spoke to the dogs.

The old man casually lifted his arm and waved toward the young man. "Hello, Ryan. This is Miss Stimmons. She's from the paper. Going to write a story for the historical society that may help sell this place."

Ryan put his arm around the old man's shoulder and gave him a hug. "Miss Stimmons and I *bumped* into each other at the paper—literally. She nearly knocked me on my keister."

The old man slapped his knee and laughed out loud.

Stacy blushed, "I'm afraid I was extremely careless."

"We didn't get a chance to exchange names. I'm very glad to meet you, Miss Stimmons." Even though he had seen her at the paper, she didn't fit the picture of a reporter. She didn't wear glasses, her hair wasn't in a bun and there was no pencil behind her ear. Her tailored black-and-white hounds-tooth suit accessorized with the red bag and high-heeled shoes were too fashionably coordinated. The perfect makeup, nails and coiffure just weren't the typical image of a female reporter. No, she didn't fit the mold at all.

She extended her hand and said, "I'm very glad to meet you, Mr. Townsend. Please call me Stacy. I'm sorry this beautiful place has to be sold."

He brushed the dark hair out of his eyes and shook her hand.

"So am I, but I'm just getting my practice started. There's no way I can afford to keep it." He studied her eyes carefully.

"Ryan, why don't you show Miss Stimmons around?"

"Be glad to, Uncle Josh."

"My legs aren't what they used to be." Josh turned to ascend the steps and called over his shoulder. "Take her around the grounds and the stable, then come on up to the house. I'll get Annie to make us some coffee."

"Just let me get some flat shoes out of my car and I'll be right with you," Stacy said.

Ryan watched her intently as she picked her way

back over the crushed rock of the walkway in high heels. She moved nicely and her soft voice was a real killer.

As she returned, he noticed the flats were also red. This girl planned ahead. Her dark curls bobbed in rhythm with the skipping motion she made. She had lost height with the change of shoes making her look even younger—almost childlike. Her big dark eyes and how they danced fascinated him. Her smile, in no way, looked childlike. She was beautiful. The emotion wrapping itself around the pit of his stomach caught him off guard. He stared at the ground, kicked over a mushroom and under his breath, "Damn," escaped his lips.

"We'll begin with the rose gardens," he said, pointing in the direction of the side yard.

Stacy fumbled with the pad and pen as they walked. Why did he make her insides tremble? She took a deep breath. The two slowly strolled through the yard and out into the back gardens.

"These gardens were my aunt's pride and joy when she was alive."

The garden was overgrown with weeds now. Deadwood needed to be pruned from the bushes, but several of the plants sported beautiful blooms in spite of the strangling weeds. The air was fragrant with their aroma. Stacy took in a deep breath and let it out slowly. "Just smell," she said.

"Yeah, nice isn't it? Aunt Sue won almost every garden award there is for her roses. She grafted two bushes and came up with this apricot one with the ruffled edge. She named it after her mother, Elizabeth Galloway. They call it Liza Flare."

"It's beautiful." She bent to inhale the scented flower. "It has a wonderful citrus-like perfume."

The stable came into view. Stacy's mouth dropped open in astonishment. The workmanship and quality couldn't be matched in today's market. Ryan slid the huge double doors open. The floors were brick, laid in a herringbone pattern. The stalls were dusty but the wood had the patina of fine furniture. The hardware was solid brass.

"My granddad and his father had some of the best racing stock in Louisiana for years. Won the Kentucky Derby twice. I've forgotten how many races in New Orleans. They say the stable was even used for great parties in those days."

"This is the most beautiful stable I've ever seen."

She could almost hear the music and the noisily raucous laughter of men who had imbibed a little too much. She envisioned the oversized aisle-way full of dancing fun loving people. Ladies in beautiful silk and satin gowns twirled to waltzes and lifted their skirts to enjoy Cajun music, as well. Men engaged in good-natured boasting about their horses. How they'd have taken that race if their horse hadn't been "quicked" or

the track hadn't been wet. Women shooed away dart-
ing children playing tag between tables laden with delicious food. The children's fingers swiped across beautiful cakes to snitch a taste of frosting as they ran.

Ryan leaned against the gate of a stall. A slight
smile floated across his mouth as he remembered the
summer his cousin Jacqueline had come to visit. He'd
lost his boyhood and gained his manhood in that stall.
Jacqueline had been three years older than him and
attended an all-girls boarding school up East. Since
then, there had been other girls he'd brought to the stable in his youth, but the first was the memory he trea-
sured most. Hidden somewhere in that smile, Ryan
secretly wondered how Stacy would look with hay in
her hair and that perfect suit rumpled.

Stacy strolled through the stable, jotting notes in
her notebook as she went. When she'd finished, they
walked up the path to the house.

"You seem very close to your uncle."

"Uncle Josh and Aunt Sue raised me. My parents
were killed in a car wreck when I was nine," he said.

"I'm sorry," Stacy said.

"Aunt Sue taught me my manners and Uncle Josh
busted my britches if I didn't use them."

Stacy giggled softly.

"Those two prodded and encouraged me through
school. They paid for all the expenses that went with it,
including law school at University of Virginia. That's

part of the reason why he can't afford to keep this place now." Stacy detected guilt in his voice.

In an attempt to lighten the subject, he added, "Uncle Josh said he thought I'd be a fine lawyer because I was always looking for the loophole in anything he told me to do even when I was a kid."

"Law school is a terribly big expense these days but I can tell he's proud of you."

"He and Aunt Sue never let me know what a hardship it was on them. Oh, I could see this place wasn't being kept the way it'd been in years past. I thought it was because they were both getting up in years and just didn't have the interest anymore."

He snapped off a rose and handed it to her. "I worked part time at the university teaching business law, but that didn't begin to cover the expenses. Neither one of them had a great deal of education but respected those who did and made sure I knew its importance. People don't come any better than those two."

Stacy sniffed at the blossom and paused along the path to turn and face him. His sad dark eyes devoured her heart. "You were fortunate to have someone that cared so much," she managed softly.

"Yes, I was. My aunt died three years ago. Uncle Josh certainly does miss her. I'd give anything if he didn't have to give up this place at his age."

Ryan looked down at the ground and kicked the

dirt to avoid making eye contact again. "I'm certainly glad she can't see it."

"He told me the taxes are too much for him to deal with," Stacy said.

"That's true, but from what I've been able to find out in Baton Rouge, there's more to it than that. A man by the name of Terrace Moody is pushing hard for the state to condemn it. The talk is that they want it for a state park and wildlife sanctuary, and are particularly interested in the wetlands."

The reporter in Stacy was aroused. There might be more of a story than she originally thought.

"Then there's the historical value—whatever that's worth. Moody is using the situation as a platform to get elected on. Also, his owning the adjoining property may have a little something to do with it."

"Moody? Isn't he running for the Attorney General's office?" she asked.

"Yeah, he's the one."

"Wasn't he accused of getting mixed up in a drug scandal in New Orleans? Something about being paid off by the Mafia not to prosecute?"

"You've nailed him, all right."

Ryan observed Stacy closely. She was certainly up-to-date on local politics, but then, that was her business. It surprised him that he talked so openly with her. This wasn't something he did with friends, and certainly not a stranger.

Excitement snapped in her brown eyes with the discovery of the plantation. Her delicate features looked like a child's on Christmas morning tearing the paper off presents in anticipation. Somehow, in the questions she asked, he saw the plantation as if it were a new experience for him also. She had aroused the love he held for the old place, something he hadn't thought about for a long time. Maybe he'd just refused to acknowledge it because he knew he would have to give it up soon.

"What about you? How'd you get to be a reporter?" he asked.

"I grew up in Texas and dated the paper boy," she quipped.

He laughed. "Seriously, I can't understand what would make someone like you even want such a life. It's hard work, long hours, and certainly not glamorous."

She wondered what he meant by *like you.* By the time she had gathered her wits for an answer, they'd reached the front verandah of the house.

Stacy's heart dropped to her knees when they stepped through the portal. She was sure her eyes deceived her. A huge Waterford crystal chandelier hung in the entry adorned with a few cobwebs. The colors of the walls and draperies had faded with time but their richness could still be felt. As they moved from room to room, Ryan answered her questions. She

19

wished the rooms could talk. There were questions she wanted to ask but they wouldn't be in keeping with the reason she was here.

The library was Stacy's favorite room. Maybe that was just the writer coming out. Beautiful old leather books lined the shelves and were covered with dust. Although they had not been in use for a long time, it was evident that sometime in the past, someone possessed a love for fine books. There was a cozy fireplace and she thought how wonderful it would be to sit by the fire on a chilly, rainy day and devour the books.

Ryan looked slowly around the room and remembered the past. "Grandmother Grace spent a lot of time in here before her eyes went bad. She made sure I sat at that desk every afternoon until my homework was done. And when I couldn't play outside, she and I would sit in here and read to each other or play board games. When she died, Aunt Sue took over." Ryan smiled. "Between them I couldn't get by with anything."

"I'll bet you were spoiled rotten." Stacy smiled when she said it, but regretted it immediately. She didn't know why she'd allowed herself to make such a personal comment.

Ryan grinned sheepishly, "Yeah, you're probably right." The forthright comment told him she'd say what she thought. He could respect that.

"Great Grandmother Marjorie brought most of this

furniture back from England. The dining room furniture was her favorite. We've kept all of it—until now." His voice trailed off. He'd hoped his own children would gather around that table someday. Now it would never happen.

"The original furniture was made by freed slaves out of oak and cypress growing on the property. Most all of those pieces were given to the family of the craftsman who made them to make room for Granny Marjorie's purchases. Annie still has a few pieces her grandfather made for this house."

Ryan ran his hand over the seat of a dining chair. "Each of the Townsend women added their own touches through the years. Grandmother Grace did all this needlepoint."

"That's a lot of time and work. I can understand how they must have loved this home."

"My mother did some of the paintings throughout the house. There's two I want to keep."

Uncle Josh called. "Annie's got the coffee ready. Y'all come on in here." Ryan led Stacy into the drawing room.

An old stoop-shouldered black woman shuffled into the room carrying a large silver service. The smell of the warm spicy bread filled the room, reminding Stacy of the pumpkin bread her mother always made at Christmas.

"Oh, Annie," Ryan said. "You didn't forget my

gingerbread."

"Mista Ryan, this is Thursday, ain't it? How could I forget your gingerbread? You always come to visit on Thursday. And you like that gingerbread since you wuz a chil," Annie said affectionately, exposing the whitest teeth Stacy had ever seen. "Mista Ryan used to run through my kitchen and swipe hot gingerbread off the table when he thought I wasn't looking." She gave Ryan a big-eyed scolding look.

"It tasted better, if I stole it." Ryan laughed. "And Annie always seemed to turn her back at just the right time."

"We couldn't do without Annie," old Josh said. "She's looked after the Townsends since she was a girl. Her whole family worked on the place. Her great-great grandmother's people came with my folks from Virginia."

"Why didn't they go north like so many others did after the war?" Stacy asked.

"The Townsends took good care of their Negroes. No family was ever split up once it was established on Townsend property and they were treated fairly." His eyes snapped with pride. "They saw the bluebellies burn their homes as well as the Townsend plantation. They saw them get liquored up and rape in gangs. That's what happened to Annie's great-great-grand-mother. After that, they didn't want any part of the North."

"I can understand," Stacy said quietly.

"They came as freed slaves and with the promise of a piece of land of their own if they would help with establishing the new Townsend plantation. They got it, too, along with wages for the work they did." He nodded his head in the affirmative.

"Is Annie the only one left?" Stacy asked.

"Yeah, she stays to take care of me. She's got kids in Houston and Dallas. They've asked her to go live with them. She don't want to go. Wants to die right here." He paused. "Hell, we'd both die here if the damn state would leave us alone." His voice trailed off.

The inquisitive mind of the reporter came alive. "What do they propose, Mr. Townsend?"

"They want me to deed over four hundred acres of the swamp land for a wildlife refuge and park for the public. They been after that land for the last ten years. They say old Jean Lafitte roamed this swamp and it has some historical value." His eyes blazed. "Wildlife refuge, hell. Where do they think I'm going to hunt and fish? I'm taking better care of that ground than they would."

He took a sip of the hot coffee. "They'll bring in conservationists and engineers to build roads, buildings, and God knows what else down there in that bog. All the wildlife will leave or be killed in spite of their conservation talk. I'd as soon see it sold off as destroyed." The old man's voice cracked.

Stacy swallowed hard and stared into the fragile bone china coffee cup. She could think of nothing to say that would make the moment easier for the old man. She sensed that Ryan had the same dilemma. She looked up at him. Ryan's eyes glistened with dampness for the old man but he didn't say anything. Any sympathy added just now might seem like pity and diminish Uncle Josh's manhood. Even though she had seen the two together for a short while, she knew in her heart, there was no way that Ryan would hurt his uncle's pride.

Stacy gathered her things and rose to leave. "I believe I have enough information to write an article that will raise a lot of interest in your property, Mr. Townsend. When do you plan to conduct the auction?"

"I think I can get everything in order by the twenty-first of September. That falls on a Saturday. The weather should be cooler and hopefully the rain will hold off." The old man dragged the back of his hand across his nose and said, "If you need anything else, call Ryan. He handles all my business now and I trust him to know if he thinks it's right."

Stacy held out her hand for the old man to shake.

He took it into both of his. "I thank ya for your help, young lady, and I'm sure the article will be fine."

The sun was setting when Ryan walked Stacy to her car.

24

"Do you have a card, Stacy? Just in case, we think of something else."

She pulled a business card from her bag and handed it to him. "I'm in the office from nine to five on most days, unless I have an outside assignment." She smiled. "They'll know how to get in touch with me and thanks for the tour."

He glanced at the card and read aloud, "Stacy Stimmons," and with a grin, ad-libbed "Girl Reporter."

Stacy was set back by the little jab. Her pupils narrowed to pin points. "How big do women grow where you come from?"

He chuckled out loud at her snappy jousting. This one wasn't going to put up with any nonsense. "By the way, you still haven't told me how you became a reporter." His black eyes were cool and penetrating.

It was evident by his tone and demeanor that he was used to having his questions answered and fast. Stacy gazed straight into his eyes and knew she fascinated him and decided a little wondering wouldn't hurt him at all. She got into her car and smiled sweetly into his dark eyes, and being intentionally mysterious, lowered her voice, "No, I haven't, have I?" Turned the key and drove away.

Chapter Two

The car snaked its way out of the swamp, onto the freeway towards New Orleans. Stacy grappled with her story. Already seeing the lead and knowing the history, the description and mystique could be compelling. The story would write itself but a pit in her stomach told her something else nagged at her. The defeated look in Josh's eyes and the helplessness in Ryan's preyed on her.

It was obvious the old man didn't want to leave his home and Ryan had said he didn't want to sell. At the same time, both men knew selling could be more profitable than having the plantation taken by condemnation. The reason she'd wanted the story—to expose the desecration of historical lands seemed less important at the moment. Ryan was young enough to rebuild a life but not Josh.

She wished she'd never recognized the bared emotions. Sensing them made her weak and if she was going to succeed she couldn't afford weakness. She meant to be a professional, didn't she? Her silly sentimental feelings couldn't get in the way.

She stretched her arms, one at a time, and tried to work out some of the fatigue. The day had been long and she was, as granny always said, bone tired. A good nights sleep would help. She'd begin fresh tomorrow.

Once home, she made a tuna sandwich and settled into a steaming tub. The excitement and tension began to melt. She slipped between fresh white sheets but sleep didn't come. She couldn't get Ryan Townsend out of her mind. Those smoky dark eyes seemed to see more than they should and his Cheshire-cat grin suggested he knew something she didn't. Uneasiness stuck in her chest and she took a deep breath to release it. She was sorry for his problem but didn't have to make it hers.

She was in the office early. By three o'clock, she had the article completed to her satisfaction. In fact, she was rather proud of it. Her phone rang.

"Miss Stimmons, this is Ryan Townsend. Uncle Josh and I were looking through some old photographs last night and we found several pictures of the house. We thought you might want to use them with your article."

"Wonderful. I'd like to see them and the story's done."

"That's fast work. I'd certainly like to read the article."

Stacy immediately wished she hadn't told him that the story was completed.

"Would it be possible for us to have dinner this evening at Arnaud's? I'll bring the pictures."

Stacy glanced around the newsroom with a combination of excitement and uncertainty. Was this mixing her professional and social life? But then, this could hardly be called social. It would be the only time she'd need to see him. The auction would take place and that would be the end of it.

"Yes, Mr. Townsend, I think that's a workable plan," she said in her most professional voice. "Would seven-thirty fit your schedule?"

"That's fine. Would you like me to pick you up? And by the way, the name's Ryan. Mr. Townsend is my uncle."

"No, Ryan." She emphasized the name. "I can meet you there." No way was she falling into that trap. She'd found out in college once how it felt to be stranded somewhere with an amorous drunk on her hands. "I'll see you there at seven-thirty. Good-bye." She hung up, telling herself he was only interested in getting the old place sold.

She arrived at Arnaud's at precisely seven-thirty.

People late for appointments were one of her pet peeves. It was a dead giveaway about how responsible and serious they were about their job, not to mention plain bad manners. She wondered how Ryan Townsend would measure up.

Stepping inside the door, she inhaled the wonderful aroma of the fine Cajun cuisine. The restaurant hummed with activity and cheerful voices drifted from the main dining room. Stacy felt her stomach flutter with anticipation as she asked if Mr. Townsend had arrived.

A tall young man escorted her through the bustling room. The forward wall was mirrored making the room appear twice as large and echoing twice as many glistening crystal chandeliers. Philodendron spilled over the balcony of a second floor dining room. Dark rich woods covered the walls and were decorated with small brass plaques engraved with names.

Stacy spotted Ryan sitting at the back of the room. He put down his drink and waved toward her. She ran her hand over her hair to tame whatever the wind had tousled and approached the table. "I hope I haven't kept you waiting."

"Not at all." Ryan rose and waited for the young man to help her with her chair. "What will you have?"

"A glass of Chardonnay, please." She settled into her seat.

"A Chardonnay for the lady and another Wild

Turkey and water for me." He pushed a manila envelope across the table to her.

Carefully she spread the pictures over the table. "These are wonderful, Ryan. Look at this one with the loaded cotton wagon in front of the house."

"Yeah, Uncle Josh said he could remember those wagons making trips back and forth to the gin. His job was to ride on top of the cotton—to make sure it got there." Ryan chuckled. "See the little kid behind the mule's leg? That's Josh."

"He certainly looks like a mischievous little rascal, doesn't he?" Stacy said, grinning at Ryan.

"That's his mother on the verandah in the long white lace dress and her hair piled on her head."

"She was a beautiful woman and that dress was a dream. I think the clothes were prettier then."

"Sound as if there's an old-fashioned girl hiding in there, Stacy."

"Oh, I just like clothes. I didn't have them growing up and I'm trying to make up for lost time. My credit card bills tell me I just may do it, too." She laughed. "Do you know the black man holding the mule's bridle?"

"That's old Mose, Annie's father, grinning from ear to ear."

"Old Mose had a wonderful smile. Now I know where Annie gets those sparkling white teeth."

"That's Annie sitting on the mule."

Stacy laughed, "Look at that hair. I definitely think we should use this one."

"She and Uncle Josh have been together a long time. It's going to be distressing the day Annie leaves the place. I'm not sure how he will react. I'm worried."

"I'm sure you are. Sometimes I get a little angry with God. You'd think after the strain and struggle people go through just to survive to reach old age, He would make it a little easier for them. Instead, old age only seems to make it worse. It doesn't seem fair."

"No one said it would be fair, Stacy."

The reality of his statement brought her mind back to the business at hand. Why had she said that? It wasn't like her to get philosophical with a client. Regaining her balance she said, "I definitely think we should use this one."

"Yeah, I think it's the best of the lot. You said you had the article finished. I'd like to see it."

She flinched but reached into a mahogany-colored attaché case and handed the printout to him. "We don't normally let anyone read our copy until it goes to press, but I don't know why you shouldn't see it. It is, after all, your family's property." He took it and began reading.

Stacy studied his face as she sipped her wine. In the dimmed light, his eyes were so dark they appeared black. They looked a little sinister, certainly mysterious, but with a soft twinkle as well. His jaw had a set about it that indicated he was a no-nonsense person. He probably possesses a stubborn streak as well, she thought.

He reached into his jacket and retrieved a black Waterman pen.

"I think this line should be taken out here and added here." He pointed to the sentence with the pen. "We could elaborate more on the furnishings."

His words jolted her and Stacy's heartbeat began to thunder in her head. Her temper flared. If this wasn't the typical, "I know what's best, little lady" male response. She was all too familiar with the species. She'd worked too hard for her credentials and she knew her business. She wasn't going to be demeaned and he might as well know it right now. The tone she took was professional and matter-of-fact, but forceful. "It's not the policy of the paper to let anyone except the reporter who wrote the article rearrange. . . ."

As if realizing his blunder, he interrupted her just before she showed the really ungenteel side of her nature. "This is a good story, Stacy. I'm sure Uncle Josh will be pleased." He replaced his pen in his jacket.

"Let's order something sinful." He motioned for the waiter, "Frank, we're ready to order now."

Stacy already knew what she wanted but now her stomach churned. She wasn't sure it would stay calm.

A small misunderstanding shouldn't ruin the whole evening, she told herself. She regained her composure and ordered the Pompano en Croute with a Watercress Salad.

"That sounds good. I'll have the same and we'll have a bottle of Vouvray please."

"Excellent choice. Thank you, Sir," the waiter replied and disappeared.

"Will you be at the auction, Stacy?" he asked.

"Yes, there were some lovely things. One painting I particularly liked. I'm still in the process of decorating my condo. That painting would be stunning over my fireplace," she said.

"Which one?" he asked.

"The one in the library. It was of a beautiful brunette woman in a peach-colored dress standing with the chestnut gelding under the big oak tree."

"That was my mother. She was quite a horse-woman."

"Oh, I didn't know. Of course, you'll be wanting to keep that painting and you should."

He nodded. "How long have you been working on your condo?"

"Seems like forever. I'm not sure if you ever complete the job. It's kinda like life. It keeps growing and changing or dies."

Ryan studied her features as she talked.

"I suppose I'd be disappointed if it did get finished.

I couldn't continue to shop then." She laughed out loud trying to keep the conversation light as well as the mood.

Dinner arrived and neither was disappointed. Stacy was sure the aroma of the fish dish alone would add five pounds but she didn't say so. Ryan was devouring his with enthusiasm. The white wine was perfect with the rich creamy fish dish.

"So you appreciate antiques?" he asked popping a bite of fish into his mouth.

"One of my passions. I took a few courses in college as part of my electives. Spend my weekends searching out the shops in New Orleans and surrounding area." Stacy took a sip of wine and let it sit on her tongue for a moment. "Some of the best finds I've made have been at auctions such as the one your uncle is going to have."

Just then, a noisily festive group that had obviously started their evening early drifted through the dining room. Ryan glanced up in the direction of the disturbance. A grin started at the corners of his mouth and traveled up to his eyes like a brush fire taking off. A tall sophisticated redhead swayed her way to their table with the kind of smile that got there before she did. She snatched a sideways glimpse at Stacy, trying to size up the situation—or the competition. "Well, hello, Ryan. I heard you were back in the area."

Ryan stood and took the gorgeous girl by the hand

and planted a solid kiss on her cheek.

"Danielle, it's good to see you again. I thought you were living in New York and vowed never to set foot in crawdad country again."

"Well," she drawled in a slow honeyed tone, "the glitter of New York turned out to be a little blinding; however, the shopping was wonderful." Her laugh was musical and clear. One any well-born southern lady could be proud of.

"Danielle, I'd like you to meet Stacy Stimmons. Stacy's a reporter with the *Picayune*. She's writing an article on the plantation for the historical society membership drive. Uncle Josh is selling the plantation, you may have heard. Stacy, this is Danielle Derusseau. I'm sorry," he said shaking his head. "I mean Danielle Parker, I keep forgetting you're a married woman now."

Stacy extended her hand and said, "Glad to meet you, Mrs. Parker."

Danielle smiled, took the hand absent-mindedly, shook it and turned back to Ryan. "I was sorry to hear the old place was going up for auction. We had some fun times out there, didn't we?" She leaned into Ryan nudging him playfully with her shoulder.

Stacy knew the familiarity meant that they were more than "just friends." But then she was sure Ryan had known a great many girls—and women. It was obvious this one certainly had all the old southern charm Daddy's money could buy.

Danielle looked up to see her party being seated in the next room. "I must be going. I'm with friends. Listen, Roland and I am giving a party out at the house on the twenty-fourth. Do come and bring your friend." Danielle motioned towards Stacy. "We can talk about old times and make Roland deliciously jealous."

She sashayed through the tables to a private dining area. Ryan's eyes were glued to the back of the jewel-blue beaded cocktail dress being flounced to perfection. Danielle turned to make sure he was watching and blew him a kiss over her shoulder showing the pearly whites once more. They had worked their magic. Ryan seemed to have lost his composure.

Stacy thought he was making an even bigger ass out of himself by trying so hard not to appear smitten by the rear end of that blue dress.

"Care for desert or coffee?" he offered, pulling back his gaze.

"No, I'm satisfied, thank you."

"Well, I suppose that about does it unless there's something else you need?"

"No, I'm sure I have all I need. You can expect to see this in the paper the week before the fourteenth of September," she said. She slid her chair back and rose to leave, feeling as if she had been dismissed like a child from the dinner table. Her eyes stung with humiliation. She was sure he wanted to join Danielle and her friends for the evening—or maybe the night if Roland Parker wasn't in town.

Whoa, what's wrong with me? Why shouldn't he have wanted to join his friends? She certainly didn't own him. Own him? She didn't even like him. Being as objective as possible, she tried to analyze why she was so upset? Jealousy? Ridiculous.

Early the next morning, the phone woke her. It was Ryan. "Stacy, if you don't have plans for Saturday night, I'd like to take you to the theater and dinner."

She heard, in the tone of his voice, an apology for the last evening's abrupt behavior but she wasn't buying it.

"I'm sorry, Ryan, but I have plans for Saturday."

"How about a drive Sunday afternoon and dinner at Commanders Palace?"

"No, thank you. I have plans for Sunday also, but thank you for the invitation. Good-bye." She hung up the phone before he could make another attempt.

The rest of the week seemed to drag. She covered a couple of dinners for the social column and put the finishing touches to the articles she was writing for the historical society. She didn't hear from Ryan again but then, she didn't expect to. She had been rather short with him but he'd deserved it.

Saturday morning arrived. She gave a long lazy groaning stretch, enjoying the coziness of her covers.

Today she could do what she wanted. Stacy put on some old jeans and a faded red tee shirt. She tied her dark hair back and started on the project for the weekend—painting the living room. She had chosen a golden peach color that changed tones as the sun moved from east to west.

Midmorning the doorbell rang. She climbed down the ladder to answer it with paint roller in hand and with a good deal of annoyance for the interruption.

Ryan stood in the doorway with roses advanced. "A peace offering." He smiled, not doubting for a moment that they would be received warmly. "What are you doing?" he asked, taking note of Stacy's well-fitting jeans. He laughed. "You've got more paint on yourself than the walls."

Stacy wasn't amused. "Mr. Townsend, I'm in the middle of a project and now is not a good time to receive visitors and I'm allergic to roses. If you hurry maybe you can get your money back."

He had already laid the flowers on the dining table and was pulling off the corduroy sport jacket. He took the paint roller out of her hand.

Stacy promptly took it back.

"Oh, come off it, Stacy. You're steamed because of Danielle. I confess I made a fool of myself the other night."

Stacy planted her hands on her hips. "You're doing the talking."

"I' m trying to say I'm sorry. It wasn't that way, but I can't explain."

"Ryan, I know a good turn-on when I see one and you were all but bellowing like a bull."

Ryan grinned sheepishly but was smart enough not to offer any further defense.

Stacy continued to fire. "Not to mention that I thought you were rude. You dismissed me from the table as if I were a child. It was more than a little obvious that you wanted to join *Mrs.* Parker's party." She emphasized the fact that Danielle was a married woman in the event he had forgotten.

"You're right, I did want to join her party. But not for the reason you think."

"Want to explain it to me?"

"I can't just yet. Listen Stacy; you and I were just getting to know each other. I'd like to be friends." The pleading in his eyes told her he was sincere. Rolling up his sleeves, he said, "We can finish this in half the time if we both work at it."

Stacy plopped the paint roller into his hand and smirked sweetly at him. She went to the kitchen for a vase for the flowers. She could use a good friend but he was certainly going to have to earn it.

In less than two hours, they were finished. The color turned out to be even more beautiful than she anticipated. The contrast of the peachy tone with the white woodwork was just the right softness she wanted and the apricot colored brick of the fireplace made the room stunning. Still, she needed to find just the right painting to go over the fireplace. She knew exactly where it was but it was definitely out of reach now.

"Why don't you get prettied up? I'll finish cleaning up this mess. We'll drive across Lake Pontchartrain for dinner," he said.

She took a quick shower and couldn't resist choosing a jewel toned blue dress. She stepped into the kitchen just as he was finishing with the last of the cleanup.

"Nice dress," he said. "You look great."

"Well, I recall you seem to like blue," she jabbed.

"Ouch. Guess I had that coming," he said. "Let's call a truce, Stacy, and start over."

"Agreed," she said, extending her hand for him to shake. Instead, he raised it to his lips and kissed it, catching her completely off guard. *Damn him. He thinks he's really slick.*

The evening was humid, but was cooling off to pleasant for August in New Orleans. The sun slid slowly behind the clouds and the sky radiated color. Pinks, purples, and blues blew across the heavens.

Stacy drew her breath in to smell the last bloom of the honeysuckle. The air was perfumed with it. She watched the brown pelicans diving into the lake for their dinner as *Stardust* played on the radio. She remained quiet for most of the drive. She couldn't help but wonder what "old friend" was going to show up at this restaurant.

"Good evening, Mr. Townsend," the maitre d' at Broussard's welcomed them. "I have a nice table on the water side if you would like."

"Sounds fine, George." Ryan took Stacy's arm and guided her to the table.

Looks as if he makes this watering hole regularly also, Stacy thought. Beyond the large glass windows, sailboats glided over the lake with their sails rippling in the wind. The water glimmered with the last remnant of the sun. Stacy absorbed the tranquillity of the scene and felt the tightness in her shoulders relax. They sat down and perused the menu. She was more interested in absorbing the surroundings than the printed list of foods. "Why don't you order for me since you're familiar with the menu?"

He ordered gumbo for an appetizer, a salad, snapper stuffed with crab in papillote, puffed potatoes, and accompanied it with a bottle of Sancerre from the Loire Valley of France. For a struggling attorney, frugality doesn't seem to be a priority she thought. Maybe he's trying to impress me. More than likely, that was it.

He returned the menu to the waiter and focused his attention on Stacy. "You still haven't told me how you became a reporter for the *Picayune*. I would have guessed something to do with fashion or decorating. I saw your flare for the latter today."

"What do you mean?"

"The color you chose. How did you know it was going to look that great? That takes some knowledge." He chuckled as he pointed to her hair. "Looks like a bad highlighting job."

She removed a compact from her purse. Paint meant for the walls were laced through some of her dark strands. She lifted her hand in an attempt to banish it. It was dry and not going anywhere.

"I think it's a lost cause," he said. "Besides, it's cute. Don't worry about it."

Stacy shrugged realizing there was nothing she could do.

"Where'd you grow up, Stacy?"

"In a swampland area of East Texas known as the Big Thicket. My dad worked in the oil refineries along the coast."

"Where did you go to school?"

"I graduated from Vanderbilt."

"Vanderbilt? That's a long way from Texas."

"That's what my dad thought too, but I was lucky enough to receive a scholarship. He only had a sixth grade education, so he was proud of me."

"How does anyone make it with only a sixth grade education?"

"Not very well. That's why he understood its importance and let me go. His mission in life was to make sure that his kids got a high school diploma."

Stacy eyes softened. "Somehow there was always money for paper, pencils, and books, but no way could I have gone without the scholarship. I worked nights as a switchboard operator at the hospital for the extras I needed."

"Why New Orleans?"

"Minored in history. New Orleans history has always fascinated me. I love the old homes, Bourbon Street, the mystique of the city—even the smell."

He chuckled. "Know what you mean. New Orleans has something special that's difficult to explain." Ryan ran his finger around the top of his wineglass. "Why the *Picayune*? Why not one of the magazines?"

"That's easy. Because Mitch McGalliard is the best editor in the South and I knew I could learn a lot from him." Her eyes snapped. "I want to become an editor. It's hard work, but not dull. I love it." Her eyes danced with excitement. "Then as Jenny Joseph's poem goes, when I am old and wearing purple, I will have plenty of material for novels which I will write sitting on a verandah, or is it a lanai, on some Hawaiian island."

"And, of course, they'll all be best sellers," he added.

"Of course." She laughed at herself and so did he. The ice seemed broken, at least, temporarily.

Stacy picked up her knife and buttered a bite of

bread. "Tell me, what was your uncle talking about, with regard to the historical aspects of the plantation and Jean Lafitte? Sounds like a good story."

"I'm sure you know, all the area around New Orleans was LaFitte's stomping ground. His head-quarters was on Grand Terre in the Barataria Bay. It was used for smuggling purposes, including slaves."

Stacy nodded. Anyone growing up on the Texas coast had some knowledge of Jean Lafitte.

"Anyway, legend has it that he buried treasure along the bay and swamps. There is strong evidence Uncle Josh's land is a possibility."

Stacy's interest was peaked and it showed.

"Some of LaFitte's treasure was even found as far southwest as Galveston or at least they think it was his. I understand he had a way with the ladies also."

The sly grin that had made her uneasy the day they met floated across his face again. The same mysteri-ously dark eyes probed hers. Hot and flushed, she clasped her hands tightly in her lap; hoping nervous-ness didn't betray her. Secretly, she felt the bolting impulse of a young colt. Something about this man intrigued her and frightened her at the same time.

Ryan continued with his explanation. "The National Park Service established several Jean Lafitte parks and preserves. They're always on the lookout for a way to create more. It's a great way to take land away from private owners in the name of doing 'good' for the people." Ryan shrugged his shoulders. "Who knows? Maybe it's the only way we can preserve any-thing for history and the generations that follow. I'm not so sure it's a bad thing as long as it's not your land they want." He chuckled.

"Yes, I see your point."

"I'm afraid that if Uncle Josh doesn't sell the place soon, they will condemn it and give him a pittance for it. It could happen."

"Then he'd be worse off than now," Stacy said.

"That's right."

The gumbo arrived. The hot steaming bowl of seafood smelled wonderful. It had been a long time since breakfast and lunch had been forgotten in the midst of the painting project.

The day was turning out to be more pleasant than anticipated. In fact, it had been a delightful day and she had a freshly painted living room as well. She was glad she'd accepted the invitation. She had to admit her dis-like for Ryan was dwindling. He was definitely inter-esting and possessed a sense of humor. Still, could she trust him? Something made her uneasy.

The still of the evening moved in as they drove back into New Orleans. Fog found its way across the bayous like a ghost army invading the swamp, readying its position for the night. The night sparkled from the car's headlights, bouncing reflections off night flying insects. The air was intoxicating with the fragrant aromas of jasmine or maybe the wine was better than she originally thought.

"Stacy, I keep a small sailing boat down at Ponchartrain Yacht Club. Nothing fancy you understand. It's only a thirty-five foot Endeavor. I'm planning to take her out tomorrow." He grinned. "If you haven't got another room to paint, why don't you come along? We can take a picnic lunch and head for high seas—or at least the middle of Lake Ponchartrain."

Stacy recognized the club name as the most prestigious in the area. For an attorney just starting a practice that company was expensive. "Sounds like fun but I warn you. I don't know the first thing about sailing. I can pole a pirogue pretty good."

"You don't have to do anything, I can handle it by myself. Have to admit, it's more fun with two but I bought one that could be operated alone."

"I understand that sailing is something that gets in your blood and never goes into remission," she said.

He laughed. "I'm afraid that's true. I've been sailing since I was a kid. Learned on Uncle Josh's pond in back of the house. He and I built my first little sloop. It was just big enough for the two of us."

"Sounds as if you and Uncle Josh did a lot together."

"Yeah, he didn't deny me anything in his power to give."

"I really can't afford to keep the *Jury Room* and

certainly shouldn't keep it at the Ponchartrain Yacht Club. However, in defense of my extravagance, I have met a number of politicians and acquaintances at the club who have become clients." He smiled. "I rationalize. If they own boats, they can usually pay my fees. On the other hand, maybe they don't pay my fees because they own boats."

Stacy laughed and he laughed at himself. It was buried pretty deep, but yes, he did have a sense of humor. As he drove, she observed the strong line of his jaw and straight nose. It was neither too long nor too short. He was good looking and, of course, he knew it.

"It's the one luxury I allow myself. It's been my salvation the last few years." He didn't expound. Something in the tone of his voice told her not to inquire any further.

They reached her door more quickly than she'd hoped. She retrieved her door key from her bag. "Thank you for a pleasant evening and din. . . ." He unexpectedly drew her firmly to him, pinning her arms along with her handbag between them. He cupped her chin with his free hand and gently planted a kiss on her nose. "Pick you up at eight. Good night, Stac."

Before she could regain her balance, he'd vanished into the elevator and was gone. Stacy reached up and touched her nose. She didn't mind the kiss but the snatched manner with which he took it bothered her.

From somewhere down the street the whine of the

blues floated through the apartment like smoke. She slipped into a white silk gown and pulled the sheet up under her chin. She was tired, but it was a satisfying kind of tired. The kind that makes your body demand a good long stretch. She enjoyed a lazy long groan along with it. All things considered, it had been a wonderful day. The wine had done its magic and. sleep soon overcame her thoughts.

Thunder exploded and lightning flashed across the room like fireworks going off. Gale force winds blew open the French doors of her bedroom. The curtains billowed out into the room like the spreading wings of a giant blue heron while pelting drops of rain soaked the filmy fabric. Another crack of thunder and lightning flashed.

Stacy bolted across the room to close the doors. A strange feeling crawled up her spine. The feeling of not being alone. She turned and saw a massive dark figure towering over her. A stiff heavy cover of some type was thrown over her head. It scratched her bare arms and shoulders. She was hoisted onto the shoulder of the big man. The smell of bay rum, sweat and the mustiness of the cover took her breath away. She thought she would suffocate. She could feel herself being carried down the outside stairs and onto the street. She pleaded with her stomach not to throw up inside the sack from the jolting.

With the scouring sound of sandpaper, the kidnappers hurried down the brick street. She heard the splash of water as they dodged puddles and that of heavy breathing as her attackers made their way through the street. They spoke not a word.

Finally, she was plopped onto a hard, wet surface. It swayed gently back and forth. She heard the sound of oars dipping into water. The craft moved as thunder continued to rumble. Breathing in the heavy dusty sack became her major concern.

Stacy kicked at her bedcovers fighting for just one breath of fresh air aware that she was dreaming but unable to break free from the nightmare.

"Come aboard, mate. You've got her, have you? Let's see the booty."

Stacy was set on her feet clumsily and she staggered, almost losing her balance. Forceful hands steadied her. The floor swayed and the bag, covering her head, was jerked off. Her eyes didn't focus and she blinked several times to clear her sight. The heavy canvas had rubbed her nose raw and it burned in the fresh salt air. She struggled to open heavy lids that felt sewn shut.

She was on a ship, a large windjammer. In the moonlight and mist, the ship took on a phantom quality. The sails furled, the framework of the masts gave the appearance of a skeleton ship. Lanterns loomed and disappeared into the darkness as men scurried about performing duties. Gentle waves caught the light and broke into dance on the water. Stacy gave a low sigh and drifted farther into the blurred rhythm of the ship and the mystery.

"She'll fetch a pretty picayune down on the Campeche block," one of the grisly men said. Another stepped up from behind and turned her around briskly.

"She's not for the block and you'd better not have harmed a hair on her head or you'll answer to the cat," he said.

The big man, in a heavy Scottish brogue said, "No, Capt'n Lafitte. We surprised the lass good. There was no fighting. She'll not have a bruise on her."

Ryan stood before her, dressed in black britches and waistcoat, with a white ruffled shirt—pirates attire from head to toe. His raven hair rippled in the wind and his black eyes gleamed in triumph. That inevitable, sly, all-knowing grin was pasted across his mouth. Even as her blood chilled with fear and confusion, she thought him the most handsome man she had ever seen.

Regaining her composure, she squared her shoulders and placed her hands on her hips. "What's this all about, Ryan?" she demanded. He glared at her, but didn't answer.

"Take her to my cabin," he directed her captors. "Lock the door. Pierre, you stand guard."

"I have a right to know what's happening," she

demanded.

"Keep you mouth shut, wench, or you'll have the right to feel the wrath of my hand across those lovely lips."

Stacy squirmed under the rough hands holding her. She was forced down the stairs and pushed through the door of a cabin. She caught herself on the post of a bunk to keep from falling from the force of the shove.

This was all too real. She attempted to scream to wake herself but nothing escaped her lips. She plunged deeper into the dream.

The cabin smelled of rum and the sweat of man. When had the bedclothes been washed? A single lantern swinging overhead lighted the chamber. Light flickered over the waves at the back of the cabin.

She ran to the stern window that spanned the width of the ship and heard voices overhead speaking French. Lights from the harbor dimmed as the ship moved out into open waters.

She collapsed onto the foul smelling covers of the bunk and cried uncontrollably. Knowing any show of weakness would be the worst thing she could do, she had put forward a brave and blustery face. Now, alone, she released the frustration. Why was Ryan acting this way? What did he want? Why was she being treated so badly?

The door whined loudly as it opened and Stacy sat up wiping her eyes across the sleeve of her robe. Ryan stood in the doorway with those piercing black eyes riveted on her. A sinister grin slashed his handsome face. She jumped to her feet to stand her ground.

"Well girl, what do you think of my little ship? *The Pride* has all the luxuries to make our journey comfortable. The rest of the trip to Grand Terre will be unforgettable for us both." His white teeth gleamed, as he slowly looked her over from head to toe. "You're a good-looking wench and you've got pluck. I like that in a woman. Come here." Taking her by the shoulders, he forced her towards the bed.

She stepped away from him, raising her arms to fend him off. "No," she screamed and threw all the weight of her slight build into him. He fell backwards into the closed door with a thud. He roared with laughter and plunged for her again.

There arose a round of loud laughter outside the door. "Need any help in there, Capt'n?" one of the men taunted. Her screams didn't deter him at all. He lunged at her, tearing the bodice of her gown and pulling her to him. She struggled with all her might but he held her firmly to his breast. She sank her teeth into the base of his neck. They found their mark and she tasted blood. She felt his muscles harden straining to draw back from her. He twisted his neck in an attempt to see the wound. Starring wide-eyed at it, he smiled that smug grin and drew her to him again. His mouth came crashing down on hers. Quick as a cobra strike, she took a bite out of his lip. He threw her backwards against the bulkhead. "Devil cat." He spat, spewing blood over the floor and bedcovers.

A scream burst through the fog of the dream. Stacy realized it was hers. She moaned and sat straight up in bed as another crash of thunder sounded. Her head reeled in confusion and her heart pounded with fear. She sobbed, "Ryan, Ryan. Why?" As her head cleared itself of the drowsiness, she knew she had been dreaming. *You Ninny. You're really wound up about being with him tomorrow, aren't you?* She slumped down into the pillows in complete exhaustion but didn't allow her eyes to close for fear the dream would reappear.

Chapter Three

The sun squinted through the blinds and directly onto her eyes. She tried to ignore it and turned over. Then the alarm clock rudely summoned her. She had wanted to get up early enough so she didn't have to hurry to get dressed. Now she wished she had slept another half-hour. Slowly she pulled herself free from the covers and sat up.

Coffee. She needed coffee. Thank goodness, she'd loaded the pot last night. A slight headache knocked on her brain. She didn't know whether it was last night's wine or the nightmare. She raised the mug and inhaled the aroma. The hot drink comforted her as it slid down her throat. She chased it with a couple of aspirin.

What was she going to wear? She stumbled to the closet looking for a pair of white denims; a navy striped knitted tee shirt, and a white windbreaker. Where were her white Keds? She rummaged the closet floor. No shoes. She plopped down on all fours to look under the bed and wished immediately she had moved a little slower. Her head throbbed like someone beating a tom-tom. There they are. She spied them up near the headboard of the bed. They needed a good washing. No time now.

She let her robe drop to the floor and turned on the shower. Tepid water peppered down on her head. She stood there letting the warmth bathe the back of her neck. Maybe it would help the headache go away. Wide-awake now, she felt as if she might live after all.

She took extra care applying her makeup. She wanted an outdoorsy look but with a hint of glamour, in case they went to the club later. She blow-dried her hair, dressed, and examined her image in the mirror. Not exactly an old sea dog and that's not all bad. She smiled at her reflection with satisfaction.

Ryan rapped on the door promptly at eight. "You ready?"

"Yes, just let me get my hat. The sun will be blistering today." She threw together an emergency make-up bag. Experience had taught her to be prepared for the unexpected.

"You sleep good?" he asked.

"Like a rock," she lied. If his boat had the least resemblance to a pirate ship, she was outa there.

They arrived at the marina a little before nine. The sun hadn't yet burned off the dewiness of the morning. The breeze still lay quiet. That wouldn't last much longer. The marina was beginning to come alive. Boats were already moving out onto the lake.

"A perfect day for a sail." Ryan filled his lungs with the salty air. "By the way, the company that makes those jeans should pay you to wear them." He grinned at her over his shoulder and slid out of the car.

She was glad he had gotten out. She didn't want to look him in the eye at the moment. Her face felt warm. She wasn't sure if his comment or her guilt caused the blushing. It was the exact reaction she'd wanted.

Ryan strolled to the back of the car to unload the ice chest.

"Gracious, you must have enough food in there for an army," Stacy said.

"I always get hungry when I'm on the water."

A pretty sandy-haired blonde in a light blue shirt and short shorts wandered past the car. "Hello, Ryan," she purred.

Ryan straightened up as he lifted the ice chest from the trunk to see who was addressing him.

"Hey, Peggy. How are you?" he said. The girl stared at Stacy with that look all women know—the learned art of sizing up the competition. "Will we see

57

you at the club later?" Peggy asked.

"Maybe, after we come in," he answered.

Stacy gathered her hat and slung her bag over her shoulder. Peggy disappeared down the dock. There had been no opportunity for Ryan to introduce them. She thought, maybe it was just as well. After all, he is an extremely desirable bachelor. She couldn't blame the cute little blonde for trying.

"The *Jury Room* is in slip twenty-one—down this way," he said.

"*Jury Room*? That's a strange name for a boat."

"It's where the important decisions are made," he replied.

"I see. Very appropriate." Following him over the floating walkway, she gazed at the beautiful sailboats already out on the lake and enjoyed the smell of the air off the water. She watched kids throwing bread off the back of a boat to a flock of hungry seagulls. There was something almost hypnotizing about the boats gently bobbing up and down with the motion of the water.

"They are beautiful things, aren't they, Ryan? They look like swans gliding on a pond." Stacy could feel herself relaxing as she watched the boats. Maybe this was just what she needed after a week of work.

Ryan said, "Sailing is a necessity for the stress I cope with. I think they should allow a medical exemption for it. It saves money on tranquilizers, high blood pressure medication, and physician's care." He extended his hand to her. "Give me your hand. I'll help you aboard, then you take the ice chest."

The stillness of the morning was shattered with the sound of someone calling Ryan's name. Ryan set the cooler on the dock and turned to see what the problem was. A thin young man in a white jacket with the club insignia ran towards them waving a cell phone in his hand. "Mr. Townsend, there's a phone call for you. It's Mr. Parker," he said breathlessly, handing a portable phone to Ryan.

"Thanks," Ryan said, then spoke into the phone. "Hello, Roland. Wait a minute. The static on this line is bad. I'll have to go to the club and call you back. It will take me a couple of minutes." He handed the phone back to the waiter.

"Stacy, this won't take long. Make yourself at home."

Stacy took his hand and stepped aboard. Must be something really important if he's getting called on Sunday morning, she thought. She stepped down the stairs leading to the galley. It was compact but functional. She opened the microwave and closed it. She was surprised to find a set of dishes in the cabinet that looked feminine. They were a blue and yellow floral pattern of Noritake. They went perfectly with the color scheme of the tiny cabin. A blender and crockpot were stored in the cabinet. Stacy wondered if Ryan knew how to use a crockpot.

She located the small confined head. *Thank good-ness.* That small problem had been worrying her. She took advantage of the facility and her privacy of the moment. She enjoyed exploring the small vessel on her own. It was like the playhouse she always wanted as a kid but didn't get. She opened the door of the forward compartment. It revealed a mini cabin with a double bed covered by a blue spread with yellow and white pillows thrown on it. There was scarcely room to walk around the bed. It was cozy. Shelves of books lined the wall. Pictures of Ryan, the boat and a pretty blonde decorated one side of the small cabin. *Well, you knew he wasn't a monk.* She closed the door quietly.

Ryan was hurrying toward the boat when she reached the deck. "I'm sorry. Clients don't usually bother me on Sunday but this was important."

"If you need to tend to something, please do," she said. "We can sail some other time."

"No, it's not urgent. I have a meeting set up with him for tomorrow morning. That's soon enough. Let's get out on the water before the sun gets any higher."

He handed the cooler over to her, untied the lines and tossed them aboard. With one agile bound he followed. The pony motor started on the first crank. The small craft moved slowly through the harbor and out onto the open lake.

"Take the food down and secure it. Think you

could make some java. There's a coffeemaker under the sink."

"Aye, Aye, Sir." She saluted and lifted the chest. It wasn't heavy, just big for her small build.

"Put it in the blank space under the cabinet," he called down.

She pushed the chest into the empty space and located the pot along with a sack of Community coffee.

She returned to the deck with two mugs of the brew. He took a slow cautious mouthful. "That hits the spot," he said. "We'll get well away from the dock and the traffic before we put up the sails."

The warmth of the sun beaming down on her back made her feel snug and comfy inside. She took a careful swallow of the coffee and sat down on a cushioned space to watch him maneuver the boat. *He likes control.* Stacy could see it in the masterful way he ordered the little boat to perform instantly, something about the set of his jaw and the purposeful gaze in his eyes. She wondered if he was that way about all things.

The sun began to beat down a little strongly. Stacy hoped she had put on enough sunblock. Perspiration beaded on Ryan's face. He whipped off the Ralph Lauren tee shirt to soak up the sun. His chest glistened with the dampness on his skin. He was more muscled than she thought he would be. He appeared slender in his clothes. She concealed the excitement stirring within her. The wind blew through his black hair causing it fall into his eyes. He looked like a proud little boy having way too much fun. She hadn't noticed how white and even his teeth were until now. That infernal grin always seemed to take precedence. He did have a heart-stopping smile. She felt a tingle quiver over the back of her neck.

He cut the motor and set the cup into a holder. As he unfurled the sails, the boat seemed to take on a life of its own. The sails filled with wind and skimmed across the water at a much faster pace. The feeling was instantly exhilarating, so free and exciting. She hadn't expected such a feeling. Stacy took in a big deep breath of the cool wind and let it out slowly, understanding why he loved sailing so.

"Why don't you stand at the 'pulpit'? You can really feel her move up there," he said.

"Where?"

"Up there, on the front of the boat. Where that railing is."

"Okay, here goes." Stacy climbed up on the hull of the craft. She started to stand up, but reconsidered it. Her balance didn't seem sure enough for her to be comfortable with standing just yet. She inched her way out to the point on all fours and was content sitting there on the point.

He cupped his hands around his mouth and hollered. "Stand up and hold on to the rail."

Slowly she pulled herself to her feet, but held on for

dear life. Once standing, the feeling was wonderful. The boat rose to the peak of each wave, then suddenly dropped to the bottom. It was like being on a bucking horse, only smoother and more evenly paced. The water sprayed back over her. The wind took her hat off. It flew over the back of the boat and bobbed in its wake. Now her hair was beginning to stick to her head.

"Come on back," he shouted. "We'll go get it."

She inched her way back down the hull of the boat to safety.

"I think it's a lost cause, Ryan. I'm sure it will never be wearable again."

"We can hang it up. It will dry in no time. At least, it will keep that pretty little nose from getting burned today," He hung a gaff over the side and snagged the hat. He wrung it out and secured it to the jib. "Hey woman, get in that galley and make us some sandwiches."

"What have we got?" she asked.

"Turkey, ham, cheese, all the fixings and potato salad."

This she could handle. She made the sandwiches and arranged them with the potato salad on plates. She found a large tray under the cupboard. Placed the lunch on the tray and retrieved two fresh drinks. She proceeded up the stairs topside.

Ryan reached out, "May, I hel. . . ?" It was too late. Stacy's shoes slipped. The tray was air borne. Ryan grabbed for Stacy to keep her from falling. Both went down landing in potato salad that had already found its way to the deck.

"You okay?" he asked.

"Yes, just embarrassed. What a mess. I'm so sorry, Ryan. I think the soles of my shoes were wet. They certainly slid out from under me." She scooped a glob of potato salad off her shoulder that had oozed its way over her back.

Ryan began laughing. "You look good in potato salad." His black eyes locked onto hers. He pressed his weight into her and brought his lips firmly over hers. His tongue gently forced its way between her lips. He felt her tremble. He made no effort to let her go but held her close gently and whispered, "Stacy."

She held her breath and didn't try to free herself from his arms. The boat flew on its own and so did Stacy's heart.

Suddenly, as if he had remembered something, Ryan pulled her up right, "You know, we could starve to death like this."

"I think there's enough to make more sandwiches. I'll see what I can rustle up," she said.

"Guess I'll clean up this mess," he said raising his eyebrows at her. "And for God's sake, don't touch the pecan pie," he teased.

She looked back over her shoulder and gave him a "go to hell" look. He laughed out loud at her.

Stacy managed to come up with two more sand-wiches and scraped the bowl of potato salad. The morning activities had made Ryan hungry. He tore at the sandwich almost savagely. "There's enough for another is you want," she offered. He nodded yes because his mouth was too full to answer. She made another one and took it up to him. Then she went below to assess the damage in a mirror. Her shirt had become stiff with the dried potato salad. Her hat looked as if it had been first prize in a dogfight. The combination of mist from the waves and the hairspray left her hair sticky-straight and plastered to her head. Mascara smudged under her eyes made them look like she'd been in the same dogfight and lost.

She smiled at her messy reflection. Ryan had smeared crimson lipstick all over both of them but she wouldn't complain about that. There was no way she could repair the damage. She hoped he wouldn't want to go to the club later.

When she emerged on deck again, the sky had turned to late-day pink and lavender. By the time they reached the dock, the sun was sinking into the lake.

"You want to have dinner at the club?" he asked.

"Ryan, would you mind if we went on home? I look awful."

"I think you look great, but there'll be other times for the club. Frankly, I don't want to share you."

"I have two London broils in the freezer. How

does that sound?" she asked.

"Hey, you've got a deal, Lady. We'll stop and get a bottle of wine."

The sixtyish, balding, and pudgy guard unlocked the lobby door and grinned. Both were sunburned, windblown, and frazzled. "You two look like you've had quite a day."

"We have for a fact, Fred, I've just had my first sailing lesson," Stacy said. The two disheveled sailors hauled their battered bodies through the lobby.

It was the first time the guard had seen Stacy in such disarray or looking so radiant. Every morning she came down the elevator looking as if she'd just stepped out of Vogue, greeted him with a smile and a cheerful "Good morning, Fred." Every evening she returned in the same condition. She never looked as if anything happened to her in between. That was not the case this evening. He smiled. The two disappeared into the elevator.

"Ryan, if you don't mind, I think I'll take a quick shower. I'll feel much better without the potato salad."

"Sure, I'll chill the wine and defrost the steaks."

She emerged from the bath, feeling much cleaner and smelling of gardenias. The cool water had soothed the raw feeling of her sunburned face. Her cheeks needed nothing but a light powdering to cut the glare. Fresh mascara and a whisk of lipstick, she was good as new. Stacy slipped into a pink pant and tee shirt set that looked like silk but wasn't. Her Scottish background made her far too practical to wear silk in the kitchen. It was polyester and could be popped into the washer if need be. Most of all, it was light and airy and soft against her sunburned skin.

Ryan gave a low catcall whistle as she stepped into the kitchen.

"You look like strawberry ice cream," he said.

"Thank you, I think," Stacy said.

He had found items for a salad and already put it together. Steaks sizzled on the grill. Stacy popped two sweet potatoes into the microwave, set the timer and began to lay out the silverware for the table.

He planted a kiss on the tip of her sunburned nose. "I didn't know you have freckles. I like them. They make you look like a little girl. You need to get in the sun more often, Stacy."

"I hate them. I usually keep them covered with make-up."

He poured two glasses of Merlot, which they sipped as the steaks cooked. The smoky aroma of the steaks searing made Stacy's mouth water. She hadn't realized how hungry she was. Then she remembered that most of her lunch had landed on the deck. She hadn't felt like eating after embarrassing herself so. She was grateful that Ryan had been so good-natured about it.

"Thank you for asking me sailing today. I haven't done anything like that since I got to New Orleans. I think the stress of the office was getting to me."

"My pleasure."

"I haven't felt this relaxed in months. It was just what I needed"

"We'll do it again if you promise not to mess up my boat." He grinned.

Stacey refused to acknowledge the tease. "You like lime on your sweet potato?" she asked slicing a lime onto a saucer.

"I don't know. Haven't tried it."

"Makes the potato sweeter."

"If things get any sweeter around here, I'm not sure I will be able to control myself," he said as he swung his arm around Stacy's waist and gave her a hug.

The phone rang destroying the mood. Stacy picked up the receiver. "Hello. Yes, this is Stacy Stimmons. Yes, he's here. Just a moment." She handed the phone to Ryan. Who would know that he was here?

"Yeah, I understand. Tell him I'll be right there." He hung up.

"Stacy, I'm afraid I'll have to go. Something has come up. Roland needs to see me right away. I'll call you."

"Certainly. I'm sorry you can't stay. Thanks again for the lovely day."

He was gone.

The next morning Mitch walked through the news-room to his office, stopping at Stacy's desk. "Can you come into my office? I need to talk to you."

What have I done now? She picked up a tablet and followed him into his office.

"Sit down. I have an assignment for you."

Stacy released the deep breath she'd been uncon-sciously holding and allowed herself to relax deeper into the chair.

Mitch picked up a pen from his desk and pointed it at her. "This assignment is confidential. You can't dis-cuss it with anyone but me. You understand?"

"Certainly. Whatever you say."

"I'm not going to beat around the bush, Stacy. It's dangerous. It will require you working pretty close to some questionable people in order to get the informa-tion we need. What you say could cost you your life."

Stacy's felt her stomach flip flop. Mitch was wor-ried.

"These guys would put your cold body in the swamp in an instant. It's that controversial and dan-gerous."

"This sounds like a chance to work on something important."

"Hold on, there's more you need. . . ." The phone interrupted him mid-sentence. He answered it. "Yeah, I think that will run concurrently," he said into the receiver. "Just a minute." He put his hand over the receiver. "Stacy, let's have lunch and finish discussing this. Say about eleven-thirty?"

Stacy glanced at her watch. "I'll be ready."

They left the office promptly at eleven-thirty and drove down into the French Quarter to Galatoire's. Parking was difficult; but the reputation of the restaurant was worth the trouble. Mitch whipped his Lexus into a cramped space.

Stacy was eager to learn what the new assignment was. She'd been unable to sit still all morning. They ordered and while they waited for the food Mitch began to explain.

"We have a lead on a gentleman from New York, a financier of sorts. His name is Roland Parker. From what I hear, he's charming, smart and sophisticated, but mostly slick."

"Roland Parker? Roland Parker? Where have I heard that na. . . ?" Then she had it.

"He's working overtime on being accepted into the 'right' circles here and getting to know the right people politically and socially. Married a New Orleans girl. An old substantial family by the name of Derusseau."

Stacy mentally raced through the events of previous days and felt uneasy as coincidences fell into place.

"Mitch, I was with Ryan Townsend Sunday evening. He was called away from dinner for some important meeting with Parker and he introduced me to

Danielle Parker at Arnaud's."

Mitch looked squarely into her eyes with his jaw set. "Our source tells us that Parker is connected with the Mafia and is heading a drug ring here."

The whisper scratched across her throat. "A drug ring?"

"The stuff comes in from Columbia by boat and transferred by refrigerator trucks to New York. He's careful that none of it is put on the streets here. This is home. Source says he's had a couple of boys killed who tried to dump it here."

Stacy said nothing. Her heart beat in her throat.

"I don't want you to take it unless you understand what's involved and are willing to take the risk. If you turn it down, it won't reflect on your career as far as I'm concerned. You're new and you're a woman."

He could have said anything but that. There was no hesitation in her voice or eyes. "I want it."

"Stacy, if you're caught—well, you know. You sleep on it tonight and let me know in the morning. I want you to be sure."

No doubt lingered in Stacy's mind. She knew what she had to do. "Why are you offering this assignment to me?"

Mitch forked in a bite of stuffed flounder. "When I sent you on the Townsend story, I didn't know anything about this. Ryan Townsend runs with the influential crowd Roland Parker is trying to gain acceptance into and you've been seen with Townsend, so I suppose you've become friends."

"My connection to Ryan, so that's it."

"Stacy, this puts you in position of finding out what we need to know in order to expose the whole rotten barrel."

"Is Ryan Townsend involved in this?"

"We have no proof, but he may be the consigli'ere for Parker in the New Orleans area. We just don't know, but you must operate as if he is and Stacy, be very careful."

Apart from helping her career advancement, there was another reason why she couldn't turn it down. If Ryan was involved, she had to know it before she got any more entangled with him. If he wasn't, he was in danger. She might be in a position to discover facts that could protect him.

When they returned to the office, there was a message for her to call Ryan. She dialed the number and waited for his secretary to answer.

"This is Stacy Stimmons. I'm returning Mr. Townsend's call."

"Oh yes, Miss Stimmons. One moment please."

"Hello, Stac. I wonder if you would like to accompany me to the party Danielle Parker is giving on the twenty-fourth. She did invite you, too."

Stacy couldn't believe her luck.

"Why yes, Ryan, I'd love to. She seems like quite

an interesting person." Stacy wondered if Danielle Parker was involved or even aware of the business her husband was in.

"I'll pick you up at seven-thirty and Stac, please don't wear blue. It's not a lucky color for me." She heard him chuckle on the other end.

"I'll see what I can do," she said and returned the receiver to its cradle. She walked to Mitch's office and rapped on the door.

"Ryan Townsend just called and invited me to a party at Roland Parker's."

A grin was forming on Mitch's face. "You're not wasting any time, are you?"

"I'm just as surprised as you. It seemed too good an opportunity to pass up."

"Take the afternoon and go shopping. You'll need the right feathers for this party. The paper will pick up the tab." He grinned, then quickly added, "Within reason you understand."

"That's generous of the paper. There's nothing in my closet that will fill this bill," she said.

"It's not generous. It's good business. I expect to make back every penny and more."

Stacy left the office and headed for the Canal Place Center. Her mission was to acquire the prettiest, sexiest dress she could find. She made it her personal challenge to not only be seen at that party but to be accepted as a regular in the group.

She found exactly what she wanted at Saks Fifth Avenue. It was a beautiful shade of peach chiffon that made a cloud surrounding her petite figure. The color enhanced her deep chocolate-colored hair and made her eyes appear darkly mysterious. She questioned whether the deep V neckline exposed too much. The sales clerk assured her the soft alluring look was exquisite. The gentle nudge was all she needed. Stacy knew she looked good. She bought the dress.

As Stacy stepped on the escalator, to resume her search for the appropriate accessories, Danielle Parker was coming up. Danielle looked as if she'd spent the night in the beauty salon. A hair dared not stray from its assigned position. Her navy suit was impeccably cut. No doubt designer couture made specifically for her figure. Stacy guessed Oscar de la Renta. The navy was beautiful with her auburn hair glinting with touches of gold.

Stacy felt the joy of finding her own dress fade. Her enthusiasm for shopping instantly waned. She remembered the gleam she saw in Ryan's eye as Danielle left the table. She wanted him to look at her with that fire and she was going to make sure he did the night of the party. Danielle absent-mindedly stroked a toy poodle in her arms and didn't seem to see Stacy.

Just as well, thought Stacy. By this time of the afternoon in the New Orleans humidity, she felt as if she were drooping. She certainly couldn't compete with Danielle's bandbox freshness. Stacy noticed two men standing close and behind Danielle on the escalator. They were both good-looking men in a rough way. Stacy placed the ages between thirty-two and thirty-eight. The blond with a crew cut and blue eyes was well over six feet tall. The other, also tall and well built, had reddish hair and brown eyes. Their bodies looked as if they had taken up permanent residence at Gold's gym. Both were snappily dressed and seemed to be acutely aware of their surroundings. They didn't look like shopping companions. Stacy stopped at the bottom of the escalator and glanced back. Danielle handed off the little dog like a football to the blond bristle-headed man.

Stacy resumed her search for accessories on the first floor. She found a pair of silk peach pumps that she knew were far too expensive; but the color was a perfect match. She couldn't resist. She was sure that was all she was going to spend until she saw a beautiful evening bag. It wasn't a Judith Leiber, but a good copy. Depositing her Visa card on the counter once more, she vowed it was the last item. "I can't let Ryan Townsend put me into bankruptcy," she muttered to herself. She wasn't certain what Mitch had meant when he said "within reason." The sales clerk responded in that stilted tongue they are so well known to possess. "Pardon madam, did you say something?" Stacy was sure they must have to pass a test in order to prove they have acquired the condescending tone before certain establishments will employ them. "No, nothing. Thank you for your help," she said.

Passing Mrs. Fields cookies on her way to the garage, the aroma of the cookies baking enticed her. She thought about the dress and the party and decided on a nonfat cup of café au lait. She sat at one of the little tables and went over her list of purchases to make sure she hadn't forgotten anything. She needed to make an appointment to get her hair and nails done. She'd better make it right away or it would be impossible to get in on Saturday. She jotted a note to herself.

Her mind was still in a quandary as to why Danielle would be with the two men in Saks. The only plausible explanation was that they were bodyguards. From what Mitch had told her of Roland Parker, he could certainly afford guards for her. And in this day, with all the jewelry she was wearing, it was probably smart. Imagine, not being able to buy a pair of panties by yourself. Doesn't fit my lifestyle, she thought.

The next morning, she went straight to Mitch's office.

He glanced up from a stack of paper. "How did the shopping trip go?"

"Got everything I need. Now we just have to wait until Saturday night."

"So you're going through with it."

Stacy nodded.

"I thought so." Mitch seemed edgy, which was unusual for him. Stacy had never seen him quite like this. He'd been involved in the exposure of a lot of crime stories. In this business, risk and danger were not strangers. Why was he so nervous?

"Stacy, we've been informed a shipment of cocaine is coming in from Columbia Sunday night. It's going to be unloaded on dock twenty three of the Barracks Avenue Wharf."

"What are they bringing it in, Mitch?"

"A shipment of Mahi Mahi. The bags of coke are stuffed inside the frozen fish. The shipment will be transported to a New York restaurant owned by a financial partner of Mr. Roland Parker. This is it, Stacy."

"I'm as prepared as I'm going to get, Mitch."

"We have to be there when that shipment is unloaded. The New Orleans Narcs have already been put on alert. They're hoping Parker is foolish enough to show up for the transfer since he's responsible for it on this end. They want the 'Big Fish' so to speak. Pardon, bad humor."

They both grinned nervously. "Stacy, there's still time for you to back out of this. No one will know and it won't reflect on your record, I promise."

"No way. I wouldn't miss this for the world. I have sort of a personal interest now and I have to know the truth about someone."

"Have you got a gun? I want you with more protection than a camera and ball-point pen."

"Yes, I took the handgun training program and qualified for a permit. Don't worry, I can use it if I have to."

"Okay, I'll pick you up at your place at twelve o'clock sharp. Dress warm and tie your running shoes on tight, Kid. You're really going to have a busy weekend."

It was difficult for Stacy to keep her mind focused on anything but the drug bust. But she must be relaxed Saturday night. She knew Ryan would read it in an instant if she weren't. She dreaded knowing the truth and yet knew she had to. "Please God, don't let it be true."

Chapter Four

Saturday seemed to come much too quickly. The visit to the salon had been a nice experience, easing the tension somewhat. Her hair turned out just the way she'd envisioned. Once home, she laid out peach silk underwear, the sheerest hose and her dress making a mannequin with the articles to double check that she hadn't overlooked anything. All must be perfect.

She barricaded herself in the bathroom and took a long relaxing bubble bath, enjoying a glass of white wine before dressing. She spent an extra half-hour on the makeup. Tonight she would even put on false eyelashes. Her dress floated over her head and came to rest covering her diminutive body perfectly. She looked in the mirror and was pleased with the results of her work and planning. To her way of thinking that was all it was—work and planning. That she possessed natural beauty never entered her mind.

At seven-thirty, the doorbell rang. She smiled to herself, checked her image once more in the hall mirror and opened the door. She heard Ryan take in his breath as he scanned the vision.

"Stacy, you look gorgeous," he breathed soft and low. He didn't have to say anything. His eyes told Stacy exactly what she wanted to know. She had clearly set him on his heels. He moved toward her to take her in his arms. She dared not let that happen. She knew she'd be unable to say no if he ever touched her. She turned and hurriedly gathered up her wrap and bag. "I'm ready, Ryan. We can go," she said.

"How was your week?" she asked, attempting to pull his attention away from her.

His smile faded. "I spent most of it in Baton Rouge. I have a client down there engaged in acquiring a large tract of land. The negotiations keep changing, so the contract has to be continually updated and he wants me to wave my hand over it at every step."

"That would mean a lot of work for you, wouldn't it?"

"Every time a lot is sold to some poor sucker who's willing to hang a thirty-year mortgage around his neck, they need a lawyer to draw up the papers."

"I see." Now she had a pretty good description of

what he thought of home and marriage. Considering the circumstances that loomed, maybe it was just as well, she thought. Stacy had made up her mind that the best way to get through the evening was to keep it as light as she could. She knew playing the giggling empty-headed bit of fluff wasn't going to make it past Ryan, but she could be pleasant.

The conversation seemed to die and the air almost crackled with tension between them.

Ryan wished he could take back the casual comment he had heard other attorneys use when in the company of each other. Somehow it hadn't been nearly as amusing as he remembered. He could hardly keep his mind on finding the Parker's old plantation home. He tried to keep his eyes focused on the yellow stripe down the center of the road; but, every so often his gaze would wander sideways to capture a glimpse of the vision beside him. His brain wouldn't let him dismiss how desirable Stacy looked or how much he wanted to feel the warmth of her body and the sweetness of her mouth. He wondered if she knew the effect she had on him. He hadn't felt so alive for a long time but she didn't need to know it. It was only fair that she should know marriage wasn't in his plans and that crack should do it. With the way she looked tonight, he needed to remind himself, also.

Stacy decided she was glad he'd dropped the bomb. It would put distance between them. If he were involved in Parker's scheme, it would be easier to forget him. She had no intention of complicating her life with marriage, either. But if he was mixed up in this mess, how could she bear it?

Finally, she broke the silence. "How is Uncle Josh doing?"

"He and Annie are working themselves to death trying to get the place looking sharp for the auction. I'll have to say it looks better than I've seen it in a long time. I think they're both trying to keep busy so they don't have time to think about it. I've got one other angle I want to investigate before that auction takes place. It may lead to nothing so I haven't told Uncle Josh. I don't want to give him any false hope if it doesn't work out."

"I understand." Stacy squirmed in her seat. The tight merry-widow under her dress was not the most comfortable item to wear. "How far out do the Parkers live?" she asked.

"Not far now. Her father bought the old Taylor Plantation for them as a wedding present. Probably to make sure Danielle would always have a home regardless of what Roland did. Pretty smart old man." The last comment hinted that Ryan held his own opinion about Roland Parker. He didn't elaborate and she didn't pursue it.

The house was coming into sight through moss-laden trees swaying in the breeze.

"Do you know the old Indian myth about why moss grows in the trees?" she asked.

"No, but I bet you're going to tell me."

"Yes, I am," she replied smugly. "A beautiful Seminole Indian princess died of swamp fever. Her lover cut off her braids and spread them in the tree he buried her under. They turned gray with time and hang in the trees now as a reminder of their love forever. How do you like that?"

He smiled at her. "I like it."

The car pulled into the circular drive. Lanterns glowed around the drive and hung in trees. Every light in the house must have been on. The huge white house looked like a perfect square. Six massive pillars supported the second and attic floors on the front of the mansion. They continued around the other three sides of the home. The pillars provided a large verandah all around the house—upstairs and down. Three dormers jutted out from the roof and atop it all, a widow's walk. The setting could not have been improved on.

Ryan asked, "How many pillars are around the house, Stacy?"

Carefully counting the front pillars, she replied, "There's twenty-four."

"Where did you go to school? There's only twenty," Ryan corrected. "The ones on the ends support two sides."

"Of course. Why didn't I see that?" she said. She

knew exactly why. Her mind was on Sunday night and the drug bust. What kind of revelations it would bring? She closed her eyes tight and took in a deep breath to ease the tension.

"I'll bet you don't even know which two are farthest apart?" A smug smile crept across his mouth.

Stacy looked at the long porch for several seconds. "They all look evenly spaced to me."

"The ones on each end," he chuckled.

She smiled. "O.K. smart ass. I can tell this is going to be a long night."

Smiling in return, Ryan focused his dark penetrating eyes straight into hers. "God, I hope so."

In an attempt to sidestep that remark, Stacy said, "The Parkers must have an army of gardeners. The landscaping is impeccable." Most of the manicured area was done in large azalea bushes. A huge rose garden lay off to the left side of the herringbone brick walk. A garden to the right and of equal size was done in camellia bushes. Flowering shrubs and border plants lined the walkway. The notes of *Moon River* drifted through the still humid air of the evening. They could see couples dancing through the sparkling windows. It was like stepping back in time.

"What a beautiful place, Ryan," she said.

"Yeah, I'd like to see Dawn's Promise restored like this. It could be just as beautiful. It takes a lot of hard work and a lot of money to make a place look like this.

More importantly, it takes someone to do it for—and with," he added. "For and with" hung in the air like an unfulfilled promise.

Stacy dared not track the last comment.

He helped her from the car. They ascended the steps and reached the front door. He gave her hand a last squeeze before they made their entrance. The door swung open to another world. Percy, the black butler, greeted them. He was small in stature but the beaming smile gave him the presence of a mountain. He radiated warmth. He was bald on top and hair around his head gave him a halo of white. Dressed in his formal attire, he made a striking appearance.

"Good evening Percy."

"Good evening, Mr. Townsend. How are you this fine night?" the old black man asked.

"Couldn't be better, Percy."

"Yes Sir, I can see that," he grinned, acknowledging Stacy's presence on Ryan's arm.

The home had the most beautiful interior Stacy had ever seen. So many of the old mansions had a dark, dusty look, making them depressing. But this house was alive with color, plants, and gleaming crystal chandeliers. Caged macaws screamed, announcing the arrival of each guest.

Stacy had been chosen by her journalism professor to accompany a group of art students to France her senior year. Her assignment was to write an article covering the trip for the university paper. When she saw her work in print, she was hooked on the newspaper business.

She saw Monet's paintings at the Louvre and Giverny, his home outside Paris. She was sure two of his originals hung in the entrance foyer of the Parker home. The mansion was overrun with Chippendale antiques. The dining room was done in a beautiful hand painted Chinese chinoiserie. Danielle had good taste.

Danielle and Roland Parker had stationed themselves near the front door to welcome their guests. As usual, Danielle was stunning. Stacy could feel herself recoil in at least lukewarm jealousy. She didn't usually feel this way about beautiful women she met, but there was just too much familiarity between Danielle and Ryan. Danielle wore a black sequined gown exposing an exquisite décolletage. Stacy wondered how she could breathe in it, much less move. *Oh hell, give the lady credit, she looks ravishing.*

Ryan stepped forward to say hello and planted a kiss upon Danielle's cheek. "You look gorgeous, Danielle."

"I'm so glad you could come, Ryan. I see you've brought Miss Stimmons. We must get to know each other," she said to Stacy.

"Yes, I'd like that," Stacy replied.

"I don't believe you've met Roland?" Roland was everything Stacy had expected, only more so. Cary

Grant had nothing on him. He was tall, athletic looking, but not too muscular. She guessed tennis and golf
were his games. The type that always looks just right
in Armani suits and Gucci shoes. The dark hair with
slight graying at the temples only added to his sophis-
tication and his searching gray-blue eyes impaled her.
He stepped forward to take her hand.

"Miss Stimmons, I'm very glad to meet you.
Danielle told me that Ryan was keeping extremely
pretty company these days. I can see what she meant.
I hope you enjoy yourself tonight."

"Thank you, I'm sure I will."

Turning his attention to Ryan, he said, "Ryan, I'd
like to see you in my study for a few minutes. You will
excuse us for a while, won't you Miss Stimmons?"

"Of course," Stacy answered. It struck her that the
conversation had been cut rather short. A hint of con-
trolled urgency invaded Roland's voice.

"I'll be back soon," Ryan said, giving her a quick
wink. He disappeared into the library with Roland.

Stacy was left standing with Danielle. Danielle
smiled. "Let's commandeer one of these waiters and
get a glass of wine, shall we, Stacy?" The two women
made their way through the dancing couples. Danielle
stopped several times to introduce Stacy as Ryan's girl.
Stacy was more than confused. She wanted to be
Ryan's girl, at the same time was perturbed to have a
label of ownership stamped on her like the Good

Housekeeping Seal of Approval. The rationale of becoming upset about that seemed to be insignificant compared to the greatest quandary of all. Was Ryan involved in Roland's scheme? How would she deal with it if he were?

By the time they had gotten a waiter's attention, she was more than ready for the wine.

Danielle asked, "How long have you known Ryan?"

"Not long. We became acquainted through an article I wrote about the Townsend plantation."

"Yes, I remember Ryan saying that the night we met at Arnaud's."

"How long have you known him?" Stacy wished she could have taken back the words as fast as she had blurted out the question. It was really none of her business.

Danielle smiled. "Ryan and I go way back. We went to school together. We played together, rode horses together and went skinny-dipping together in his Uncle Josh's pond. Ryan is quite a boy and I'm very fond of him. But that's all, so you can relax," Danielle added with an all knowing grin. Stacy smiled back. She liked Danielle much better immediately.

"Does it show that much?" Stacy asked.

"Yes dear, I'm afraid it does. I'm just glad to see him out with anyone. Alice's death was hard on him."

"Alice?" Stacy asked.

"Yes, Alice Winters. They were engaged to be married. He thought the sun rose and set in her. So did everyone else for that matter. She was a beautiful petite blonde with swimming pool blue eyes. She was smart, too."

"What happened to her?"

"She was in med. school when they found the lump in her breast. She was just too busy with school and planning her life with Ryan."

Stacy felt the floor sway a little under her feet and perspiration break out on her forehead. Now she knew the girl in the picture with Ryan she'd found on board the *Jury Room*.

Danielle continued, "You'd think someone in the field would've been more observant and cautious. I suppose she refused to believe anything could terminate their happiness. By the time she faced the reality and let anyone know—it was too late. She died within the year. Ryan was. . . . Oh, here come the boys already."

Stacy struggled to rid herself of the initial shock. She didn't want Ryan to see her misted eyes or the drink trembling in her hand. He'd never mentioned anything about Alice. Why? Maybe that was what he'd meant about restoring the plantation when he said one needed someone to do it "with and for."

Roland and Ryan approached them. Roland leaned over and said something to Danielle. Stacy couldn't hear what was said over the music. Danielle and Roland glided onto the floor. Ryan slid his arm around her waist. Why did he have to be so damned good-looking and charming?

"May I have this dance, beautiful lady?"

Stacy forced a smile and moved into his waiting arms. The music was mesmerizing and Ryan was a much better dancer than Stacy thought he would be. They floated over the floor, never touching it.

"Stacy," Ryan whispered in her ear. "You're the most beautiful woman in the room." He pulled her closer to him. She could feel his desire and it frightened her. Her mind whirled with questions. Why had Roland needed to talk to him so urgently? Tonight wasn't the time business should be discussed, unless it was something urgent. Were they discussing the shipment coming in tomorrow night? What was Ryan getting out of all this? What was his connection? As if this wasn't enough, overshadowing it all, was he still in love with Alice?

As Ryan turned Stacy around the dance floor, she noticed Mitch McGalliard standing in a small group engaged in conversation, but his penetrating eyes focused on Ryan and her.

"There's Mitch," Stacy said. "I didn't know he was going to be here."

"Yes, I'm not surprised. He and Danielle are old friends. There was talk she would marry him until her parents sent her off to meet the 'right sort.' Mitch didn't fit the picture they had for Danielle."

Stacy was a little set back. Mitch hadn't made any mention of knowing Danielle personally when he explained the assignment. Why not?

"The Derusseau family has been here since before the Battle of New Orleans. Old man Derusseau always liked to brag about his ancestor fighting along side of Andrew Jackson and being friends and business partners with Jean Lafitte. Nobody elaborates on what kind of business," Ryan said.

"Sounds like a lot of good material for a story," Stacy said.

"Anyway, Danielle's father ended up owning a substantial portion of Jefferson Parish. Danielle's always pretty down to earth in spite of being spoiled rotten. Daddy had the money and he spent it on her."

"It shows. She has wonderful taste. This house and the way she dresses demonstrates that."

"The Derusseau's thought she and Mitch were too close. Mitch was just a rice farmer's son who worked his way through Louisiana Tech. They packed her off to a fancy boarding school up North. Seems Danielle went to a New York party and met Roland Parker. The whole town buzzed for months. Evidently, Roland really swept her off her feet with the bright lights of New York. I guess the grass was just greener. I think Mitch's still carrying a torch."

They danced their way over to the group to say hello to Mitch. Stacy hoped Mitch would ask her to dance. She really needed to talk to him.

"Good evening, Townsend. I see you've captured my star reporter."

"You bet," Ryan answered. "Good to see you, Mitch. It's been a long time. This is some kind of party, isn't it?"

"Yes, but then you know Danielle doesn't do anything less than first class. I'm not going to let this music be wasted. Stacy, may I have this dance? You don't mind loaning me your girl for a while, do you Ryan?"

Before Ryan could answer, Mitch had swung Stacy onto the floor. "You look stunning, Stacy. The shopping trip was well worth the tab."

"Thanks, Mitch. From the response I got from Ryan, I think the 'feathers', as you called them, were effective. Did you know he'd been engaged to a girl that died?"

"Yes, I knew. Alice Winters was a special lady."

"Why didn't you tell me? It would have explained a lot."

"Wouldn't have changed anything, would it?"

"No, I suppose not," she said.

"Did you meet Roland?" he asked.

"Yes, Roland wanted to speak to Ryan as soon as we arrived. I don't know why, but it seemed to have an urgency about it. Have you noticed there are two men posted at every entrance?"

"Yeah, Roland's got the place secured all right," he said.

"When I was shopping last week, I saw Danielle in Saks. She was with the two standing at the south door. They seemed extremely protective."

"From what I understand, Danielle doesn't go anywhere by herself. Whether that's what she wants or whether she's not allowed to go out alone, I don't know," Mitch said.

"Do you think she is involved in this?" she asked.

"I don't know. I hope not. Her family left her with plenty money. They were highly respected people in this area. It's not like Danielle to be mixed up in something like this, but then," he lowered his voice, "you don't know what time and too much money can do."

He was watching Danielle intently. She was dancing with Terrance Moody. Over Terrance's shoulder Danielle watched Mitch and Stacy just as closely. There was genuine concern in Mitch's voice for Danielle. No doubt about it, Ryan had been right. Not only was Mitch carrying a torch, he had his own private bonfire going.

"Looks as if we both have the same problem," Stacy said. "Neither one of us knows whether the person we care about is going to be caught in the middle of this thing."

"Yeah, I guess you're right, Stacy," he answered. "I tried to forget her. Guess I'm just a one-woman man. Don't misinterpret what I'm saying. I have a high regard for the institution of marriage and I wouldn't do anything to disrupt hers. Nevertheless, I can't help how I feel about her." He hesitated then added, "But I can help what I do about it."

Stacy was anxious to change the subject. This was territory a boss and employee should forego. At the same time, she was glad he confided in her. It created a special bond between them.

"Mitch, what do you know about Terrance Moody? Ryan mentioned his name in connection with the taking of the Townsend land by public domain. From the tone, I gathered the man has a rather dubious past."

"I know he owns the property next to the Townsend place. If it were taken for a park or reserve, more than likely they'd want his also. Surprise. Instantly, his worthless bog becomes valuable. So goes the taxpayer's money. Then, there's talk he's mixed up with some pretty shady characters. Nothing has ever been proven, at least so far. That makes him lily white. Just right for running as a candidate."

"Candidate for what?" Stacy asked.

"An attorney general looking the other way when you needed him to would be just what the Mafia needs. What could be more convenient?" he asked.

Frank Sinatra singing *Strangers in the Night* came

to a gentle stop. "Thanks, Stac, and be careful."

"My pleasure, Boss."

Mitch returned Stacy to Ryan's side. "Thanks, old man. She's quite a dancer. You're a lucky man. I'll see y'all later." He disappeared through the guests.

"Ryan, I need some air. Could we go for a walk in the garden?"

"Best idea you've had all evening," he said.

The night was perfect. The moon had come up and was almost full. Peacocks sang to one another in the distance. The aroma of roses and camellias filled the air and was intoxicating. Ryan pulled Stacy from the walkway and behind a huge live oak out of the light of the house.

"Stacy, Stacy," he whispered. "I've been wanting to do this all evening." He brought her to him firmly and demandingly. He kissed her neck. Her breath quickened as he kissed the exposed portion of her breasts.

Stacy buried her fingers in his thick wavy hair and held him to her.

Moving his kisses up her neck. Ryan devoured her mouth. Parting her lips with his tongue, he claimed her soul. "Let's go home, Stac," he whispered.

Stacy didn't want anything to disturb the wonderful warm joy pulsing through her veins. At the same time, she knew she couldn't become anymore involved than she already was. She must know whether or not

Ryan was mixed up with Roland Parker—in any way. She was apprehensive about how to handle the situation. What was she going to do when they reached her apartment? He would expect her to meet his passion with her own. She had already tasted the fire and shortness of breath in her chest when he kissed her in the garden. He must have felt her tremble and knew he had stirred her. This must not go any further. His voice nudged her attention back to the present.

"Stacy, there's something I need to tell you."

"What is it, Ryan?" She braced herself for the worst.

"Stacy, there was someone in my life that I was head over heels in love with. I'm not sure I'm over it, even now. She died a little over three years ago."

"Ryan, you don't need to tell me this."

"Yes, yes, I do. I think I'm falling in love with you. I'm not sure if I ever want to care about another person like that ever again. I know how quickly love can be snatched away and I don't think I could endure anything like that a second time."

"What are you trying to say, Ryan?"

"Stacy, you really threw me off guard tonight. It's been wonderful and I want to make love to you in the worse way, but right now, I'm afraid that wouldn't be fair to either of us."

"What do you propose to do about it?" she asked.

"Stacy, I have some business in Baton Rouge to

take care of this next week. I'm not going to call. I think we need some distance for a while."

"I see. Yes, maybe it would be best, Ryan." Scalding white heat stung behind her eyeballs, but she was determined tears would not roll down her cheeks. The rest of the ride home was silent. They reached her doorway. He gave her a peck of a kiss and disappeared quickly down the stairs.

The problem of handling the arrival at the apartment had solved itself. Worry now loomed even larger, only in a different direction. What was the reason he needed to go to Baton Rouge? Would he be seeing someone else?

Chapter Five

Sleep refused to settle over her. Conversations of the evening continued to play over and over in her mind. If Ryan was mixed up in this drug mess maybe it was just as well he had pulled back from the relationship. Maybe he'd done her a favor. Why couldn't she make herself believe that?

Her mind jumped to tomorrow night and what would be expected of her. Mitch was depending on her. She must be alert. *I need sleep.* In desperation she kicked off the covers and trudged to the bathroom for a sleeping pill.

At eleven A. M. the phone jolted her to full consciousness. She hoped it was Ryan and hesitated to say hello for fear it wasn't.

"Stacy?" It was Mitch's composed even tone. "Everything's set for the pow-wow tonight. You sure you still want to do this?"

"Yes, of course. Same time?"

"Yeah," he said. "I'll see you then."

The rest of the morning, she paced the apartment in an attempt to control the jitters. When this no longer worked, she sat down to answer some letters but couldn't keep her mind on them. Picked up a copy of *Town & Country* but couldn't keep her focus on the bright magazine pages either. Finally, as a last resort, switched on the television. A basketball game flashed across the screen. Oh no, not in the mood for that she thought. Maybe a good brisk walk would relieve some of the tension.

The Garden District was lovely this time of year. Roses and daylilies still bloomed in the yards of the gracious well-kept old homes. She'd been thrilled to find a condo in an ivy covered red brick Georgian on St. Charles Ave. That it was affordable was a second thrill. Stacy picked up the pace to a slow jog. The fresh fragrance of Jasmine hung in the air and filled her lungs. Children tossing a ball shouted noisily in a near-by yard. A dog came up and barked half-heartedly to let the boss know he was on duty. This New Orleans was a world away from Bourbon Street.

In an hour she returned to the condo and checked the answering machine. No calls. Disappointed, Stacy headed for the tub taking the portable phone with her. He could at least call she thought. A long soak with Chopin and a glass of cool lemonade was needed. The tartness of the drink caused her to wrinkle her nose and set her teeth on edge. She reached for a crystal bottle of scented bath oil and dropped in a generous amount. A little pampering might make her feel better. The warm Gardenia fragrant water slid over her body. Her muscles surrendered and she closed her eyes.

Feeling refreshed and relaxed to grogginess she slipped into a terrycloth robe, and switched on the television. Even a lousy movie would take up some time.

At six, she forced a can of chicken noodle soup down and nibbled a few Ritz crackers to calm her stomach. The mug quivered and it took both hands to prevent spilling the hot liquid. She had to get hold of herself. Mitch was sticking his neck out by letting her have this assignment. Nausea swept through her stomach in a wave. *I'm not going to let him down—no matter what.*

At eleven, Stacy changed into a pair of black slacks with a warm black sweater, dark socks, and navy running shoes. With her dark hair, she wouldn't be easily seen in the night.

Digging into her handbag, she pulled out a pocket-sized tape recorder and slipped in a new tape. The camera needed film and she checked the nine-millimeter Beretta for the third time. It was loaded. She didn't want to use the thing; but vowed, if she had to, she would. The nausea retreated.

Midnight approached, Stacy stood by the window and waited for Mitch's blue Lexus to appear. The car pulled to the curb. She took in a deep breath and let it out slowly. There would be no turning back now.

On the street, Mitch opened the door from his side and let it swing open. Sliding in, she smiled nervously. His solid masculine presence lifted her spirit. On my own in this but glad he's here all the same, she thought.

He smiled. "Great night for a drug bust, don't you think?"

She didn't reply.

The car sped off into the night's dampness of thick fog. Already her hair drooped against her face. She couldn't worry about hair tonight.

"Mitch," she asked softly, "how long have you been doing this?"

"Longer than I care to admit. New Orleans always been pretty rough. There's always a story out there and you have to go get it." He brushed the lock of hair out of his eyes. "They don't just appear on the desk printed out."

"Have, have you ever been hurt?"

"Yeah, once. Just a shoulder wound. My own fault. Chief Arceneaux hollered 'Duck,' and I didn't." He chuckled. "Makes you a fast learner or. . . ."

It wasn't amusing. "Yes, I'm sure it does." Her

voice was tight.

"Don't worry. Do what you're told and you'll be fine." Mitch kept his eyes glued to the smoky street and oncoming traffic. The car lights caused a terrible glare through the fog. His eyes squinted with each passing car. The car crept toward the wharf area.

"Coast Guard's been tracking the *Tiburón* since morning. I sure hope they let it dock. If they board off shore, we don't get squat for a story."

"When do the cops show up?"

"The local Narcs and DEA are already supposed to be in position inside the wharf. Probably been staked out in there most of the day."

"Why aren't they spotted?"

Mitch shrugged. "Just look like the dock workers and mix in. No one's allowed out of the area once they get set. They don't want any tip-off to fowl up the works."

Stacy couldn't help but think of the pure hell the wives of these guys must live through each day. Not knowing when you kissed him goodbye in the morning if you'd see him at night. Not knowing if your children would have a father tomorrow.

"They're hoping Parker and his goons will go aboard to check the merchandise."

"Is that when it comes down?"

"Yeah. They'll move in at that moment and, if we're lucky, catch them red handed. That'll take care of Mr. Parker's career in the drug business. Icing on the cake, if he turns state evidence and helps expose Moody before the election." Mitch chuckled. "I'm sure they plan to offer him the opportunity."

"How do you know the plan of attack. Mitch?"

"Informant, goes by the name of Lafitte. That's all I can tell you, Stacy."

She didn't pursue the questioning any further. They reached the last block.

"Stacy, I'm going to park on Esplanade Avenue near the corner of Chartres. It's about three blocks from the wharf that the ship is supposed to dock. We'll have to hoof it from there." He slowed, cut the lights and swung the car to the curb.

Stacy pulled on her jacket and opened her bag to make sure the gun was still there as if she expected it to have disappeared. She snapped the bag shut, slung it over her shoulder and waited for Mitch to turn off the motor. As soon as he did, she reached for the handle of the door.

"Not so fast. You can't haul that suitcase around. You can't get to your gun if you need it and if you need it, Stacy. You're going to need it fast."

"I need my camera."

"Sling the strap over your neck. Put the tape recorder in one pocket. The gun in the other and, Stacy . . ." He laid his hand on her shoulder. "If you have to, squeeze it off though the pocket." He grinned nervously. "I think the paper will replace your jacket."

A soft smile crept across her mouth. *Good old steady Mitch. He's nervous too and trying to keep things light to reassure me.* She appreciated his effort; however, each was well aware of the risk.

They moved quickly and quietly down Esplanade toward the dock where the craft was expected. The wharf was enclosed inside a high concrete wall. Only one street light lit the entrance. "How are we going to get in there, Mitch?"

"Follow me and stay close," he whispered. He crouched down next to the concrete wall and led her down it to the right. "Here it is." He propped the ladder on the wall.

"How'd you know that ladder would be there?" Stacy asked. She immediately realized that she was asking too many questions.

He didn't answer her but whispered, "I'm going up the ladder and drop to the ground on the other side. It's a long drop for you, but I'll break your fall. The name of this game is 'quiet'. If you twist an ankle or break a leg, I don't want to hear a thing. Understand?"

Stacy nodded her head in the affirmative.

Mitch scampered up the ladder without making a sound and was over. Stacy strained to hear him hit the ground but heard nothing. She took a deep breath, put her foot on the first rung, and adrenaline took over.

She was on the other side in the safety of Mitch's arms. He shoved her into the shadow of the wall.

A refrigerator truck drove through the gate and stopped in front of dock twenty-three just as expected. Two figures sat in the cab. Stacy could see the outline of a hat on one. A light colored Cadillac pulled into the shadows across the parking area and cut its engine. The driver lit up a cigarette. The glow silhouetted three others inside the car.

"That must be Parker," Mitch said.

Stacy whispered, "Where are the cops? I still don't see anyone."

"No, and you won't til they tap you on the shoulder. When this starts coming down, they'll pour out of every crevice on this block. Let's just hope they don't mistake us for the bad guys. We stay out of the way until this thing is secured. You understand?"

Stacy nodded.

"See the sliding door ajar at the far end of the dock?" Mitch asked.

"Yes."

"I'm going to make a break for it and wait just inside for you. Give me time to make sure it's clear. If you don't hear anything, you follow and stay in the shadows."

"Mitch, be careful."

He moved off across the parking area into the building. Stacy waited until he was out of sight. She heard nothing and moved in the same direction she had seen him go. Inside the door she pressed her body close to the wall. A hand reached out and touched her. Her whole body involuntary jumped but she made no sound. From inside the door they could see the Cadillac and the docking area. They stood in the darkness trying not to breathe loudly. The cold dampness made Stacy's knees feel frozen. If she had to run, would her legs work?

Finally, a ship split the fog making its way up the channel toward the pier. The noise of the engines waned and roared up several times as tugboats moored the craft next to the wharf. The water beneath the boats churned like Stacy's stomach. With the racket of the tugs masking the sound, she breathed a little more regularly. Seamen moved quickly covering the deck like fire ants on a stirred mound. They heaved huge ropes to others waiting on the dock to secure the vessel. The operation was no sooner completed than the glowing cigarette in the car was flicked out the window to the ground. Four men got out of the Cadillac and walked slowly through the wharf area towards the craft.

Stacy drew in her breath, with almost a sob, recognizing the stride of Ryan Townsend. Beside him walked another man dressed in a hat and overcoat. This was probably Roland Parker. The two approached the gangplank with caution and purpose. The captain greeted them with handshakes and they moved into the shadows of the deck disappearing through the hatch into the lower portion of the ship.

The moment they were out of sight, the wharf came alive with cops and drug enforcement officers. Amazing, she thought, how quietly that many men could move though the darkness and fog. A story about the training would make a great follow-up story for later.

A shot rang out somewhere in the dark from down below deck. Stacy quit breathing. A shiver ripped through her body. *Where was Ryan?* She glanced wide-eyed toward Mitch.

"Come on, Stacy. It's our turn now. Try to get as much of the confusion on tape as you can."

She flipped on the recorder and sprinted toward the ship. Determined to stay abreast of Mitch, she half ran and half skipped to keep up with his six-foot frame. Another shot rang out. She flinched again, but this time the shot didn't catch her off guard. Her heart ached thinking of Ryan, even before they reached the *Tiburón.* She hadn't said anything to Mitch yet. The damning truth would be out soon enough.

They raced up the gangplank, onto the deck and across to the opening they had seen the officers disappear into. They could hear yelling in Spanish and orders being barked out in English. They worked their way down the narrow corridor toward the disruption. Suddenly, it became quiet and still. What was happening? Mitch placed a finger on his mouth to indicate to her not make a sound. Then voices became more distinguishable.

Parker, along with the two burly men that had been with Danielle in Saks were surrounded. Three more emerged from the shadows with their hands in the air. One of them was Ryan.

Stacy swallowed a sob as her eyes met Ryan's. How could he do this to her? She looked away.

Officers in jeans and vests with NARC across the back focused guns on the group. Chief Arcenaux stepped out of the squad of officers and faced Parker. "Well, Mr. Parker. Was your shipment of fish fresh enough for you?" Parker glared at him but said nothing.

The chief picked up a fish and ran his hand inside the white of the belly. He pulled out a plastic bag of milk-colored powder.

"Looks as if you're not going to be in the restaurant business for quite a while."

"You can't pin a thing on me. When my attorneys get through, you won't have zip," Roland said.

"Looks like one of your attorneys is in as much trouble as you are." Arcenaux glanced at Ryan.

Stacy leaned against the frame of the doorway to steady herself and kept the camera clicking. That picture would assure Arcenaux's job for at least five more years she thought. During that five years, he would have a charitable feeling for her and his blessing could help her get many good stories down the road. She was a professional and she was ambitious, probably more at this moment than ever before.

Parker exploded, "How in the hell did you find out about this? Who was it, Arcenaux? Who's the informer?" His eyes were no longer those of a man but some wild cornered animal gone mad. "I'll get the son of a bitch."

"Yeah, yeah, we know," the chief said. "Jerry, cuff these guys, read them their rights and get them downtown." The officer moved forward to place the cuffs on Roland. Roland shoved the officer back.

"You're not taking me anywhere." He broke and ran toward the entrance of the corridor.

Stacy stood in the door blocking his pathway. She saw Parker's eyes glazed with determination. The muscular body charged her. He was going through her. Two choices flashed across her mind. She could stand there and take the force of the hit or she could step out of the way. Taking the easy way out might be the smart thing to do, but it wasn't her way. Her small frame wouldn't stop him but she might slow him down. She braced herself. Her finger froze to the button on the camera and she thought just don't break the camera you son of a bitch.

Mitch moved like a propelled dart. The only thing he could get a firm hold on was her hair. She let out a yelp and sailed through the air. She and Mitch landed with a solid thud in a heap.

Roland flew past Stacy and Mitch. Pain gripped her shoulder, but she kept clicking the camera hoping she'd gotten a good picture.

A shot rang out. Roland fell.

"Jesus, Stacy, why didn't you pull your gun?" Mitch asked still holding her.

"Couldn't shoot a gun and a camera at the same time." She sat up and rubbed her shoulder. "And like you said, good stories don't just appear on your desk."

Mitch shook his head and glanced towards Ryan who was as white as the bellies of the fish loaded with cocaine.

"Get a stretcher in here," Arcenaux yelled as he bent over Roland.

Roland groaned, "Who ratted? When I find out who, he's a dead man. Tell Danielle. . . ." Roland passed out.

Mitch helped Stacy to her feet. "Stac, you okay?"

"Yeah, I think so. Bruised maybe but everything seems to work." She moved to Arcenaux's side to get one more picture of the wounded man and willed herself not to glance at Ryan.

A stretcher and medical crew came through the door. Arcenaux said, "You men better get him to the hospital fast. We don't want to loose this guy now. Sergeant Louque, ride in the ambulance with him. If he

111

regains consciousness, take down anything he says, got it?"

As soon as the ambulance team left, Mitch asked, "How does it look, Chief?"

"He's losing a lot of blood. Looks bad. Time will tell."

Stacy could feel Ryan's eyes on her and avoided meeting them with her own. She heard the cuffs snapped around his wrists. It sounded like an iron door being clanged shut on all her dreams. He was led away with others.

A single tear welled in the corner of her eye and escaped down her cheek. She brushed it away with one quick swipe and glared at his back. She hoped he'd get all he deserved.

The ambulance's siren grew fainter in the distance.

Arcenaux's voice thundered through the corridor, "Bob, have your guys search the rest of the ship and inventory the take. The rest of you, round up these sailors and get them to lockup."

"Yes sir, I'll take care of it," the officer said.

Arcenaux pointed his finger at the young man. "Be damn sure that every one of these bastards gets their rights read. I don't want this screwed up on some technicality." Putting a little more bite in the warning he added, "I'll have the guy's badge that fouls this up. You hear?"

Mitch put his arm around Stacy's shoulder. Stacy

was grateful for the strong support. Her first drug bust would be something she'd never forget—no matter how much she wanted to. The gesture demonstrated his understanding. He had been where she was now.

"Good work, Lady. Think you can make a story out of that in a couple of hours?"

She felt her world falling apart, but said, "Piece of cake."

Mitch smiled to himself and opened the car door for her. "We need to go on down to the station and make sure we understand what the charges will be so you get the story straight."

Stacy cringed. She needed some time alone to come to terms with what she had just witnessed and she really didn't want to have to face Ryan Townsend—not now. Reality kicked in reminding her if she was going to survive in the paper business, she'd face a lot of things she didn't find pleasant. She said nothing.

When they reached the station, the officer at the front desk told them that Chief Arcenaux would like to see them in his office. The officer directed them down the hall.

Mitch knocked on the door.

"Y'all come on in," the chief hollered from behind the door. Mitch motioned to Stacy to take a chair and he leaned against the wall.

From behind his desk, the chief glanced at Stacy

over his glasses and put his head down to light his pipe. "You handled that pretty good, *chérie.*" He winked at Mitch.

Stacy knew Mitch and Arcenaux had maintained a good working relationship and it had been beneficial to both. Stacy smiled appreciatively toward the chief. "Thank you, sir."

The chief was blowing his first drag to the ceiling when the door opened. An officer guided Ryan by the arm into the office and placed him rather roughly in the chair beside Stacy. Arcenaux motioned to the officer. "Take the cuffs off. I don't think Mr. Townsend is going anywhere."

The officer removed the cuffs. Arcenaux said, "That will be all, officer."

As the door closed, a grin spread over Arcenaux's face. He stood up and leaned over the desk with his hand outreached. About the same time, Ryan stood up and placed his hand in the chief's.

Stacy stared dumb-founded first at Mitch and then to Ryan "I don't under. . ." and was interrupted by the chief.

"Hell of a good job, Townsend. Roland Parker regained consciousness in the ambulance and is already singing his head off. He's implicated Moody as far back as five years. We haven't even scratched the surface but I bet Mr. Moody won't be running for dog catcher."

Ryan nodded his head in the affirmative then frowned. "But we didn't get the supplier. Did we, Chief?"

"No, but Parker gave us the name—Gonzalo Quesada."

Mitch's eyes flashed. "Gonzalo Quesada, the Colombian connection? I thought he worked the East Coast."

Arcenaux took another drag from his pipe. "He does but evidently he's expanding his territory. He's as bad as they come, Ryan. He won't let this go without retaliation."

Mitch looked worried. "Ryan, as soon as you hit the street, they're going to know you were in on this bust."

"Mitch is right," Arcenaux said. "Quesada will be looking to make an example of you. This goon has a large organization. He can't afford to let anyone betray the operation and get by with it."

"I can't spend my life sitting in this station," Ryan said.

"No, you can't and I don't have the manpower to keep guards with you," Arcenaux said. "But you can carry a gun and keep your eyes open. Ryan, you know he's infiltrated our system with his men, so trust no one."

Ryan ran his hand across his mouth. "I really wanted to put the whole bunch away, Chief."

"I did too and we will. It will just take time. What bothers me more is that your cover has been blown."

Stacy couldn't believe what she was hearing. She looked confused and glanced towards Mitch, who was grinning from ear to ear.

"I'm sorry Stacy, I couldn't tell you. It was safer for you if you didn't know. Ryan is Lafitte. He's been working with the attorney general's office out of Baton Rouge over two years to help us catch this garbage."

Stacy stared blankly at Ryan. The tension could be contained no longer. Tears tumbled down her face, but accompanied by a smile. Ryan pulled her into his arms.

"I don't get it. Dry eyed as the Sahara when you think I'm a no good son of a bitch and tears when I'm Mr. Wonderful. A guy just can't win."

The four laughed. Stacy was glad that he hadn't seen the tear escape earlier. Someone rapped on the door and the plain-clothes officer who had accompanied Roland in the ambulance stuck his head in.

"Chief, Roland Parker fell into a coma at the hospital. He didn't make it."

"Did we get his confession down before he died?"

"Yeah, we got it all."

Mitch said, "Stacy, I don't think you're going to need a ride home, so I'm going on."

"You're right. I think I can find a ride," Stacy said smiling up at Ryan.

Mitch turned to go, then stopped. "Stac, I can't proof your story. I've got something I have to do." He glanced at Ryan, then back to Stacy. "Use your own judgment and get the pictures developed. They're waiting on the story. O.K?"

Stacy looked uneasy but nodded.

"Mitch, I think Danielle will need you about now," Ryan said.

"Yeah, that's where I'm going. I'd like to be there if she does need me," He gave a silent wave in the air over his shoulder and vanished.

Ryan shook the Chief's hand once again. Placing his arm around Stacy's shoulder they strolled out into the thickness of the fog. When they reached the curb, a taxi waited for them.

"*Times-Picayune*, driver," Ryan said.

Stacy was quiet.

"What's wrong, Stac?"

Stacy raised her eyes to meet his. "I'm worried, Ryan. I'm afraid to write the story because of the danger it puts you in. I couldn't live with it if you were hurt—or worse."

"Stacy, this can't be kept quite. If you don't write it, someone else will have to and they won't do nearly as good a job. You were there. You saw it." He squeezed her hand. "Mitch sent you on this assignment because he knew you'd do whatever it took to get the story. You've got it, so write it."

"Are you sure, Ryan?"

"Of course I'm sure."

"I'm having trouble comprehending the hazards you've been living with for the past two years." She shut her eyes tightly and pressed her head to Ryan's chest. "I don't know how you've done it."

"I knew the risk when I became involved, Stacy. At the time, I just didn't happen to care. That's changed. You can believe I intend to be extremely careful. So quit worrying."

"I'm not certain I can do that, but you're right. I know I have to write the story. Mitch is depending on me. Thank you, Ryan."

Ryan took her into his arms. His mouth covered hers. His tongue gently parted her lips. He took her breath with his desire.

Recovering her composure, Stacy took a compact from her pocket and attempted to clean up her makeup. "You know, I kinda think I just might have a headline."

"Wouldn't surprise me at all." He smiled at her. "I'm going home to take a shower and wash off some of the filth I've been feeling for the past two years. I'm too wired to sleep. Why don't I pick you up at the office later and we'll have some breakfast? We have some talking to do."

"Yes, I think we do. I'll call you when I get the story done," Stacy said. The cab pulled up in front of the *Picayune.* The clock on the tower informed them it was three-fifteen. If she were going to get this in the morning paper, she would have to hurry.

At her desk, her hands flew over the keyboard. The story seemed to write itself. She reread it and with the exception of a few typos, was pleased with it.

Chapter Six

At 6:00 A.M. Ryan and Stacy sat at the Café Du Monde in the French Market. The aroma of the strong Cajun coffee wafted through the street, drawing the early morning risers in like bees to springs first nectar. The old cafe was open around the clock and a must see on every tourist's list. Stacy picked up one of the diamond-shaped doughnuts and put it down quickly, confirming that they were indeed hot. Powdered sugar covered her slacks and judging from the amount that covered the floor she wasn't the only one having that experience.

"Be careful. The coffee is even hotter," Ryan said, taking in his breath quickly to cool off his tongue.

"These are so good. Didn't know a drug bust could

make you so hungry," she said attacking another beignet.

"Stacy, slow down. You've got sugar from ear to ear. This place has been here since the 1860's. I don't think they're going to shut down before you get all you want," Ryan teased.

The morning edition had hit the street. An elderly gentleman sat at the next table avidly reading *The Times-Picayune* as he consumed his coffee and doughnuts. Ryan craned his neck to see the paper. Sure enough, Stacy had gotten her first headline. His grin and the look in his eyes told her he was proud of her.

Ryan stood. "Guess, I better go buy a paper so I can read the lies you've told about me."

Stacy continued to enjoy the doughnuts as he read. The cafe buzzed with talk of the bust and the ruination of Terrance Moody as well as Roland Parker's demise. Stacy tried to absorb the reactions of the people. So this was what it was like to be a top reporter. She liked it. She liked it a lot.

Ryan reached across the table and took her hand in his. "Stac, I think it's great you got your headline. But I don't understand why you agreed to put yourself in such danger."

Stacy was stunned. She thought the answer should be obvious. It was her job. He had done the same thing. He didn't need to know that she must know the truth about him.

He chuckled. "You trying to prove you're better than a man?"

She leveled her eyes at him. "No, not better, but just as capable as any man."

Ryan knew immediately he had said the wrong thing. He took a deep breath and let it out slowly. "There are some things a woman has no business being involved in."

Stacy felt fire smoldering in the pit of her stomach. He was as much a chauvinist as any man she knew.

Ryan continued. "Stacy, something happened last night I wasn't expecting and it really shook me. When I saw you on that ship, I almost lost it."

"Why? You know what I do for a living. This was a real opportunity for me to get my teeth into a big story. One that could move my career to where I want to be."

"I was so afraid you were going to get hurt, or worse. Then that damn shot rang out and you were in the line of fire. Stac, I didn't know until that moment how much I love you."

The conflicting emotions ripping around in Stacy's heart were too confusing. He didn't think she should be doing her job because he loved her. That was crazy.

"Frankly, you scared the hell out of me and I don't want to be a victim again."

Stacy starred wide-eyed at him. She was speech-less but now she understood.

"I never wanted to fall in love with you or anyone else—ever. But I don't have any say in the matter, Stacy. I am in love with you. And no way will I let you do something like that again."

Stacy's eyes glistened. Slowly, she pulled her hand from his. Who did he think he was? She couldn't let him dictate what she could or could not do—even if he did love her. "What makes it any different for you? Don't you think I felt the same about your being there? What gives you th. . . ?"

The scream of a passing fire truck halted her words. The deafening sound gave her time to calm her impulse to say something she might regret but the nagging uneasiness lingered.

The shrill noise waned. She said, "I'll have to confess. I thought you were mixed up in that mess. If you were, there was nothing to do but forget you."

Ryan knew by the look on her face she wasn't lying and his ego plunged.

"Ryan, I felt like my heart was being ripped out and there was nothing I could do but watch. Mitch stuck his neck out to give me the chance for this story and I wasn't going to let him down."

Ryan nodded that he understood.

"His faith in me was all that kept me from leaving New Orleans after I thought you were involved with Parker."

He couldn't help but let that little grin start.

"Stacy, Mitch and I have been best friends since grade school. He, Danielle and I played together, swam together, fished together. He's always been in love with Danielle."

Stacy's heart dipped. "Oh, Mitch." She was sorry and excited for him in the same moment. Now she understood why Mitch left the station to go to Danielle.

"When her parents sent her away to New York, I didn't think he'd make it. He went on off to Louisiana Tech. When he returned, he buried himself in that paper trying to forget her and, also, I think to show old man Derusseau that he could be successful."

Stacy laughed. "I think he's made his point. Maybe now he and Danielle can work things out. He deserves to be happy. He's earned it." She hesitated as an old thought passed through her mind. "Ryan, the first time I met you for dinner at Arnaud's, you wanted to be with Danielle. Did that have anything to do with this?"

"Yeah, I'd been trying to gain entry into that gang for months. Danielle showing up when she did that evening was the perfect entree."

"Oh, Ryan, I'm sorry. I had no way of knowing."

"Don't be silly. It couldn't have worked out better. The meeting with you was just the reason I needed to explain my being there."

Stacy suddenly felt exhausted and lifted her hand to cover a yawn. "Ryan, I need to go on home. I'm tired and I need to get some sleep." At that moment, she could have laid her head on the table and closed her eyes.

"Come on, Kid. I'll take you home." He led her to the old Chevy parked behind Café Du Monde. She fell asleep with her head on his shoulder before they got out of the parking lot. Ryan planted a kiss on her bangs.

As they neared her apartment, he gently nudged her awake.

Stacy mumbled sleepily, "I want to go out to Danielle's this afternoon and offer my condolences. I like her a lot and I do hope she wasn't mixed up in this."

Ryan threw back his head and burst out laughing. "Who do think was tipping me off so I could keep Mitch informed?"

Stacy was wide-eyed awake now. "You mean Danielle was helping you trap Roland? Why would she do that?"

"Well, I don't know the whole story; but, Danielle was being held prisoner in that house. She knew too much."

"But what about Roland?"

"From what she tells me, the love affair between her and Roland ended long ago.. She found out that she had been used by Roland just to gain acceptance in New Orleans."

"Ryan, is she in danger? The Mafia isn't going to

like her being an informer."

"Because Roland confessed, she won't have to tell what she knows. No one but Mitch and I knew she was informing and now, of course, you. I don't think any of us are going to blab it, so I think she's safe from Mafia retaliation."

"I'm sure that takes a load off Mitch's mind as well as hers. They have to work it out, Ryan, they just have to."

Mitch stood under the shower. Hot water peppered down on his head. He was drained. His muscles were sore from the tension held in through the night. *I'm getting too old for this.* The night had brought more than just the story of cracking the drug ring. His concern for Danielle was more overwhelming than he thought it would be after all these years. Had she been informed of her husband's death? How would she take it? Had she and Roland been close? He hadn't wanted to come home even for a shower, but the night had taken its toll and he needed to regroup himself before he saw her. He dashed out of the shower with a towel wrapped around his middle. Still dripping, he made his way to the kitchen to start the coffeepot. A good strong cup of java was what was needed, but the preparation would slow him down. He decided against it and returned bedroom to get dressed.

The sun was just peeking through the moss-laden

oaks when he pulled up to the Parker mansion. He hoped he wouldn't be disturbing her, but he had to be with her. He rang the bell and stepped back.

Percy opened the door. "Oh, Mista Mitch, I'm glad you came so soon."

"How's she taking it, Percy?"

"Well, she was shocked, of course, when she first got the news. She took it pretty good though. I think she's been expecting it for some time now. She's resting in her room. I'll tell her you're here."

"Percy, if she's resting, don't disturb her. I can wait. Would there be a cup of coffee in the kitchen?"

"You is what she needs right now, Mr. Mitch. You sit yourself down. I'll have Rosie bring you the coffee." The old black man disappeared through the swinging doors leading to the kitchen.

Mitch wondered how old Percy was now. He remembered the old man bringing lemonade to the swing set under the big live oak on the east side of the Derusseau home. The childhood vision of his pushing Danielle high in the swing flew through his mind. Her long auburn corkscrew curls bobbed as she laughed, begging him to push the swing higher. The slight smile faded from his face. It seemed like an eternity ago.

Rosie entered the room carrying a silver coffee service. The aroma of the fresh chicory immediately awakened his senses. The steam escaping from the pot promised a hot bracing drink and that was just what he needed at the moment.

Rosie dabbed her eyes with a handkerchief. "Mr. Mitch, sho is good to see you again."

"Hello Rosie. You're looking just as young as ever." The compliment was given in truth. He always remembered her wearing a bright tigon on her head matching her dress that she amply filled out. Her smile radiating warmth and ever present. Everything about her was as he remembered, but today the smile was absent.

"You'll be a real comfort to Miss Danielle, right now. She's gonna need yo strength. Things ain't been easy for her, Mr. Mitch. You sit right here and enjoy your coffee. She'll be down shortly."

"Thanks, Rosie. You can't imagine how good that coffee smells to me."

"My word, I still see you children running around under the big old live oak. It's hard for a body to fathom that y'all all growed up and got the problems y'all got, " her voice trailed off as she left the room.

Mitch wondered what Rosie meant by "things hadn't been easy for her." He poured the steaming coffee into a fine porcelain cup, took one of the ham biscuits that Rosie had made and sat back on the couch to savor it.

Shortly, Mitch heard the upstairs bedroom door open. Danielle slowly descended the circular stairway. Her dressing gown was sky blue with white lace. It floated down the stairs like the foam of a wave coming home to the beach. He didn't doubt for a moment that it had come from Paris. But then all Danielle's clothes probably came from Paris. Beautiful things that he couldn't have given her. He guessed that old Derusseau had known that. That's why Danielle was sent away. A small rice farmer's son wouldn't have fitted the old man's picture at all. He wanted the best for his little girl and you can't blame a father for that.

Danielle's long auburn hair hung loose around her shoulders and she wore a blue headband matching the gown, to keep her hair from tumbling onto her face. Her eyes were red and swollen from the crying. She held herself straight and managed a small smile for her childhood friend. She walked slowly into his arms. He held her tight and rocked her as she sobbed quietly.

"You don't have to put on a brave front with me, Danielle. Cry it out. Cry it all out." He held her until the sobs quietly subsided.

"Sit down," he said. He held her hands and lowered her onto the floral chintz settee.

"Danielle, he didn't suffer long. He fell into a coma shortly after they got him to the hospital and didn't regain consciousness."

"Mitch, it's all been like a bad dream. When we first married, he was wonderful. Then things just seem to go too fast. Roland had already established himself in the banking industry; it just didn't seem to be enough." She broke into open sobs again. "Maybe I wasn't enough."

"Hush Danielle. You know that wasn't it."

"He was determined to have all the 'good things' life had to offer. He wanted that for me too—at first. That meant all the expensive things; fast cars, a yacht that would make Onasis blush, properties all over the world." She shook her head in disgust. "You name it, we owned it. Then finally, it was expensive jewelry for his expensive women. I became just one of those. He started traveling more and more without me." She pulled a lace handkerchief from her pocket. "Our marriage was over long ago. He was in love with money and its power. Not me, just what I represented. More correctly, what my daddy's money represented."

"Danielle, with some men nothing would have ever been enough. It's not the things; it's the chase. I'm sure he cared a great deal for you, Danielle."

"He always had to have the best and the newest. No matter how much money came in, even the money Daddy left me in trust went out as fast as it hit the bank. He got mixed up with the 'big boys' and their fast get-rich-quick schemes." She spat out the words.

"Danielle, it's over now."

"He got in debt to them and then they owned him. About a year ago, he began to take his frustration and his liquor out on me." Mitch's eyes bristled with anger.

"He hired body guards twenty-four hours a day to

guard the house and me. Some of the Mafia crowd started coming down here to have their meetings. I wasn't invited to sit in on those meetings, but as loud as some of them got, a vegetable would have known what was going on." Her voice strained.

"Danielle, slow down. All of this will wait until after the funeral and things are back to normal."

"You don't understand, Mitch. Things will never be back to normal."

"Take it one step at a time. You've got a lot of friends here, Danny." It had been a long time since he had used that name for her and it sounded right as it echoed from the past. "Your family still has a lot of friends here. They won't let you down. It'll just take time. And I'll be here, I have to be."

She leaned into his shoulder.

He wanted to kiss her with passion but knew that now was not the time. Slow and easy, he cautioned himself. He, also, would have to take it one step at a time.

The shrill ring of the phone nagged Stacy to open her eyes. "Go away, it's not morning yet," she grumbled. Groggily, she responded with a weak, "Hello."

"Hey, sleepyhead, this is Ryan. Wash the sleep out of those beautiful brown eyes and get some jeans on. I've got a scoop for you. I'll pick you up in fifteen minutes. Stac, be sure to wear some waterproof boots."

The phone clicked and he was gone.

The urgency in his voice immediately jolted her fully awake. She wished he'd explained. Did it have anything with the threat issued by the Mafia? Why waterproof boots?

Stacy showered quickly, jerked on jeans, a red sweater, and pulled on a pair of climbing boots. The new had been scraped off but she knew that they'd keep her feet dry. She looked into the mirror and groaned, snatched at her hair with a brush and applied a dab of lipstick. Disgusted with her appearance, she ripped a waterproof nylon jacket from the hanger. She was waiting in the lobby when Ryan's old Chevy pulled up in front of the condo. He reached over and threw open the door from the driver's side.

"Hi, beautiful," he said gathering her into his arms.

Before he could place his lips over hers, she said, "Well, tell me what's going on or did you just get me out here to neck like a couple of high school kids?"

"Both. Something's going on I don't think you want to miss and I wanted to neck with you."

She smiled and relaxed into his arms. The specter of drug lords receded from her brain. His mouth slowly covered her lips and his tongue gently played with hers. Her head spun.

Just as abruptly as he began, he released her. "Remember I told you I had something else I wanted to investigate before the auction."

"The night we went to the Parker's party?"

"Yeah, Steve Singleton, a friend I went to school with, is a geologist. He owns a company that runs seismic crews for the location of oil. Well, I decided that maybe it would be wise to find out just how much oil, if any, was under the plantation."

"What did Uncle Josh say?"

Ryan hesitated, "I contracted with him without Uncle Josh's permission. They came out and ran a seismic survey last week when Uncle Josh went to visit Aunt Sarah." Ryan laughed softly, "Shook up Annie pretty good. She thought Voodoo devils were coming out of that swamp. I told her what I was doing. She thought it was a good idea and agreed not to say anything to Uncle Josh."

"As close as they are, I know that wasn't easy for her."

"She knew there was no reason to upset him. She's always been as protective of him as a mother bear with a cub. Stacy, Steve says their tests show there's enough oil down there that Uncle Josh will never have to sell the plantation."

"Oh, Ryan." In one springy motion Stacy was across the car with her arms around his neck cutting off his air supply.

"Careful Stac, you're going to wreck us," Ryan said as he struggled to regain control of the Chevy and Stacy.

She didn't yield her strangle hold and planted a good-natured kiss on the side of his face.

"Do you think he will do it? You know how he feels about drilling on the place."

"I don't know, Stac. Uncle Josh has a mind of his own. That's for sure."

Stacy couldn't contain her optimism. "Have you told him yet?"

"No, but Stacy, that's not the best part. They were drilling a hole to place the dynamite in for the seismic testing. The guy thought he hit a tree root. They pulled the auger up to move over to try again."

Stacy had never seen him so excited. He couldn't get the words out fast enough.

"Stacy, when they brought the auger up, there was a handful of gold doubloons packed in the mud around it. They think they must have penetrated a chest."

"Lafitte's chest?"

Ryan grinned, "It's a possibility. Anyway, the crew is going to start digging at daybreak and I thought you might want to be there."

"Be there?" Stacy was having trouble containing her own excitement. "Ryan, this will be the story of the year."

"Yeah, I thought you might have a smidgen of interest."

Stacy sat back in the corner hugging herself in exhilaration. The old Chevy pulled onto the driveway of the plantation.

"I thought we'd better go by and pick up Uncle Josh."

"You'll have to tell him what you've done, Ryan."

"I know. I just don't know if he's going to like me taking the initiative of getting this done. He may feel that I was going behind his back and really be upset over it."

"Nonsense, he'll understand you're just trying to protect his interest. He's got enough of a business head on his shoulders to know he needs that information." Stacy laid her cool hand on his cheek. "Don't worry. He knows you wouldn't do anything to hurt him."

"Well, let' s hope that's the way he takes it," Ryan said.

A light was on in Uncle Josh's upstairs room and the kitchen. He was already up getting his coffee. They opened the front door and went in. Scooter, the oldest of the hounds was on their heels, determined to be involved in anything going on in his kingdom.

"Who's that?" Uncle Josh hollered from the kitchen.

"Just me, Uncle Josh. I've brought Miss Stimmons with me."

"Miss Stimmons. Good Lord, I'm still in my robe."

"I don't think she'll mind Uncle Josh," Ryan said, grinning at the old man's Victorian morality.

"Good morning, Mr. Townsend," Stacy said.

"Morning. Get some cups out of that cabinet, girl, and y'all help yourself to some coffee. Can't offer you any breakfast. Annie doesn't get here til eight."

"We'll give Annie a break today," Stacy said. "I'm cooking breakfast."

"Sit down, Uncle Josh. I've got something I need to tell you," Ryan said.

Josh pulled a chair from the kitchen table causing the legs to scrape across the floor. The two men sat down. Before Ryan could continue, the old man grinned. "Yeah, Yeah, I know, you two are getting married. Knowed it from the first day." He laughed, rocked back on the chair and slapped his knee.

Ryan rolled his eyes to the ceiling and then glanced in Stacy's direction. "No, Uncle Josh. Listen to me."

Stacy busied herself with preparation of breakfast trying to ignore Uncle Josh's perceptiveness. She dared not let her eyes meet Ryan's.

"Well, if you let her get away, you haven't got near the brains that law diploma says you have," Uncle Josh said winking at Ryan and at the same time keeping a keen eye on Stacy's back for a reaction.

Stacy knew Ryan loved her but she wasn't sure it was deep enough to sustain the kind of marriage she needed. It would take a special man to understand that she had to stand on her own feet. She was afraid Ryan wanted an "old-fashioned" girl. The kind of girl like

Danielle—always impeccably dressed with every hair in place, every gesture of her hand elegantly performed, her voice never out of control and honeyed with the proper emphasis at just the right moment. But much more than that, the kind that would let life wash over her while being content to bathe in the accomplishments of her husband.

Stacy had tasted the nectar of her own success. She thrived on it. She would never be happy attempting to be a "Danielle." She had been brutally honest with herself in facing this truth. She closed her eyes tightly and swallowed hard. She loved Ryan more than she thought it possible to love anyone. Her intestines knotted. She felt as if she had plunged a Japanese dagger deep into them committing *hara-kiri*. She was terrified of loosing him. She quickly brushed a teardrop from her face and continued to crack eggs into the pan, her back to the conversation. Stacy was jerked out of her reverie by Ryan's words.

"Uncle Josh, I did something that you may not approve of; but, you must believe I did it for your own good."

"Sounds serious, Ryan. What have ya done, boy?" the old man drawled out.

"You remember Steve Singleton? Went to school with him in Charlottesville. He's a geologist and runs a seismic company."

The old man nodded as Ryan continued, "I thought,

if we're going to have to sell this place, and we know Stafford Oil is interested in it, we might as well know why. So I called Steve. He brought out a crew and ran a seismic survey."

"Good thinking, boy. You're right."

"Uncle Josh, the report on the seismic survey indicates that there are significant pools of oil under this place. If you decide to let them drill, you'll never have to worry about money again. It means you can call the auction off."

Josh interlocked his fingers, looked down at them as he placed his hands calmly in his lap. "Ryan, all I want is to die on this place in peace. After you plant me, you can do what you want."

"Wait, Uncle Josh, I'm not finished. In one of the holes they drilled to place the charge, the drill bit brought up wood chips and gold doubloons."

"Well, I'll be damned. Sorry, Miss Stimmons," Uncle Josh apologized.

"Steve thinks they may have drilled through a chest of buried treasure. It's a long shot it'll be anything, but what've we got to lose? If it turns out to be nothing, you can still consider drilling for oil." Ryan ran his hand through his hair. "Just the negotiation and fitting the project into their timetable would probably take years." He stopped short of saying what he was thinking.

The old man didn't miss the meaning. "Yeah, it

139

would buy me time and that's all I need. A little more time." Josh laid his bony hand on Ryan's shoulder. "You're a smart boy, Ryan, and I love you," his eyes glistened with that truth.

Stacy set plates of bacon and scrambled eggs before Ryan and Uncle Josh.

Josh picked up his fork, "Smells mighty good, girl. Thank ya."

"My pleasure, Uncle Josh." It had slipped out. Calling him "Uncle Josh" as Ryan did seemed natural. Stacy placed the toast on the table and sat down to join them.

"Steve's been trying to contact me all week. I've been in Baton Rouge. Anyway, he called me late last night with the news. He's canceled their schedule and wants to start digging this morning if you say it's all right. It's kinda out of Singleton's line but he's as excited about it as I am."

"Ryan, this really takes the wind out of an old man's sails. Folks in these parts been looking for old Lafitte's treasure longer than I can remember. You bet it's all right. Where's the site?"

"Down on that little knoll that gets under water every time we have a hurricane and most of the winter. They couldn't have gotten to the knoll if it hadn't been this time of year."

Uncle Josh wolfed down the breakfast and slurped the last of the coffee in his cup. "I'll get my britches on and be right with you." He ascended the stairs and called back, "Do you think old Lafitte really killed one of his pirates and put him in with it to protect the treasure?"

Stacy shuddered. She wrapped her hands around the warm mug for comfort.

Ryan reached across the table and curled his fingers over her hands. "I haven't seen him this excited about anything in a long time. He's been just going through the motions of living until he can be with Aunt Sue again." Looking steadily at Stacy, he said, "I guess that's about the way I've been existing too until. . . ."

A loud thud from upstairs halted his words. "Uncle Josh, you all right?"

"Yeah, just dropped my danged boot."

Stacy smiled and stood to clear the table. "I better get this table cleaned up."

Ryan didn't say anything. The mood had been broken.

Stacy hoped Aunt Annie wouldn't be too upset with her for leaving the dishes in the sink.

Uncle Josh came down the stairs two at a time, looking twenty years younger than when he went up.

Ryan and Stacy amused by the old man's excitement, smiled at each other.

"Come on, Kids. Let's go," he said.

Ryan took the driver's seat and started up the motor of Uncle Josh's pickup. Stacy jumped into the truck with one smooth bound and took the seat in the middle. Uncle Josh slammed the door and the old Ford roared off.

It was still dark. The trail wound down into the bottom with its bogs. Moss hung low on the trees. It dragged over the truck cab as if trying to keep out the invaders so its hidden mysteries would remain so. Fog hovered over the bottom like a cloak shielding Ryan's view of the muddy road. The truck jolted as it fell into a hole. Water splashed up to the window, covering it with thick mud.

Stacy pitched forward and steadied herself by clasping her hand to Ryan's knee. The muscles of his leg tensed under her fingers. She quickly removed her hand and fixed her eyes on the beams of light projected down the muddy pathway. She hoped he wouldn't read anymore into her touch than it had been.

Ryan could barely see the furrows of the tires of the seismic rig in the swampy mud. Limbs had been broken over and bent by the large truck as it lumbered through the swamp. He kept his eyes glued to the ruts that guided him, but was keenly aware of the warmth that Stacy's hand had caused. He was fascinated with the paradox she presented. She always seemed to belong, regardless of the environment, be it city or the swamp. The mystery of her haunted him.

Screeching branches scraped along the side of the

truck, jogging him back to the moment. Every now and then the old pickup would bob into a deep hole and he held his breath, wondering whether the vintage vehicle could drag itself out. Red eyes stared out of the darkness into the truck's headlights. They peered momentarily to determine what was disturbing their sanctuary and then scampered off in the opposite direction.

Ryan spied lights of the seismic truck shining through the trees. Men stood around a small fire, attempting to drive away the chill and dampness that went straight to the bone this time of year. Two others gathered tools out of the back of the truck, preparing for the job at hand. Ryan hoped that Steve had told them to keep their mouths shut. They didn't need a crowd out here and it was still private property. As he applied the brakes, he saw Steve standing near the edge of the group. The three piled out of the truck and moved purposefully toward him.

"Hey, Ryan, pretty exciting isn't it? This your uncle?" Steve asked.

"Yeah, this is Josh Townsend. He owns this land," Ryan said.

The two men shook hands.

"And this is Stacy Stimmons. A friend of mine." Steve put out his hand to shake with Stacy. "You always did have nice friends, Townsend," he said. "Nice to meet you, Stacy."

"Thank you. Ryan tells me you two went to the

same school. Virginia's a long way from this bog. How did you come to settle in this area?" The reporter was still on the job.

"Oil companies pay was good for a kid just out of college. Learned what I needed to, saved my money, and when I could afford it, started my own company."

"An ambitious undertaking. I'd better let you men get to work. Nice to meet you, Steve," she said.

The fire looked inviting and Stacy strolled over to warm herself. Smoke curled its way upward through limbs and branches of pine and cypress finding freedom. Stacy took in a deep breath of the wood's aroma. The fragrance would saturate her clothes and hair. She didn't mind. It smelled like home. She said hello and introduced herself to the men standing around the blaze. Rubbing her hands together over the flames, she wished she had some gloves. Not only for warmth but also to keep her hands from being scratched by the briar vines hanging low in the trees. It was impossible to walk without moving them out of the pathway.

Somewhere in the distance Stacy heard an owl hoot and the sound carried her thoughts back to the thicket of East Texas. She remembered the early mornings she went to run a trotline with her dad and one in particular. She giggled quietly to herself while gazing into the flames.

They hadn't known the flat-bottomed boat leaked and was taking in water as they paddled out to the line.

They became absorbed in taking catfish off the line and didn't notice that water was taking over the boat until it was too late.

Daddy picked her up and threw her nine-year-old body as far as he could toward the shore. She hadn't been a strong swimmer but she thrashed her way to the bank with her Dad just behind her. They wallowed in the mud on the bank like two pigs in their laughter, the fish completely forgotten.

The priority then became how to keep Mama from finding out so Stacy could go with him again. Looking back, she realized what a dangerous situation it could have been. But she also knew it was one of the fondest and closest memories that she had of her dad.

Daylight broke. The sun glinted streams of light through the cypress trees. The swamp was waking up. In the distance, a large mouth bass made exploding splashes as he claimed his breakfast. Great egrets called to one another through the fog announcing the intruder's presence in their world. She watched a large majestic one, standing in the edge of the swamp, extend his long slim neck into the water and scoop a small fish. The swift movement was so graceful, yet deadly final. She hugged herself tight for warmth. A hot cup of Du Monde's café au lait would be wonderful about now. There was now enough light that the digging could begin. Steve's voice called out through the fog, "O.K., you guys pair up and begin digging at the point where

145

those three cypress trees intersect. You two stand ready to take over when they tire." The steady rhythm of the shovels biting into the earth began.

Steve turned to Ryan. "That drill bit must have gone through whatever the coins were in. Judging from depth of the bit ring that brought up the coins, I think it will be a good six to eight feet down."

"That's a long dig for these guys. Probably take hours before we're anywhere close."

"Yeah, I know but I don't want to use machinery. We'd better be careful as possible. I certainly don't want to damage anything if we can keep from it. It probably wasn't originally buried that deep but through the years of rising water leaving silt behind, it's about what you'd expect."

Ryan nodded and walked over to join Stacy by the fire. Uncle Josh stayed with the men digging. He didn't want to miss anything. The old man's excitement seemed more than he could contain. Ryan grinned at him as he repeatedly switched the leg he was standing on. It looked like some sort of Irish jig.

Stacy sat on a log near the fire jotting down notes.

"Stacy are you warm enough?" Ryan asked.

"I'll be fine," she answered. From the shaking of her voice, he knew she was shivering either with the dampness or excitement.

"Stac, I want you to have the story; but will you hold off until you know it all?" The penetration of his dark eyes and the way he accented "all" told her that there was more to it than just Lafitte's gold doubloons.

"I won't release anything until you say so. Ryan, where does this leave the auction? You think Josh will call it off?"

"I would think so. At least, until we find out what we've got here. That auction is the last thing on his mind right now. He looks like a kid over there, doesn't he?"

"If they do verify that it's Lafitte's treasure, it will give them a reason to condemn this land and take it for the park. Won't it, Ryan?"

Ryan shrugged his shoulders. "Might make it come about sooner, but they could take it whenever they want anyway. But Stac, we just might have an ace or two up our sleeves."

"What do you mean?" she asked.

"Stacy, Uncle Josh is eighty-five." Ryan glanced over at the old man and smiled. "Just look at him. The excitement of this thing is giving him a new reason for living."

Stacy grew impatient. "Ryan, what aces?"

Ryan grinned. "A certain person in the right political office could hold off that proceeding for quite a while."

"That's true, but I'm not related to the Governor. Are you?" she asked.

"No, but Assistant Attorney General might be a

start."

Stacy stared blankly at him. "What are you talking about, Ryan?"

"Well, with Moody making his residence at the Angola Prison, it looks like Paul Anderson will be keeping his job as Attorney General. He's asked me to be his assistant for the coming term."

"Oh, Ryan. That's wonderful. I'm so proud of you. Uncle Josh will be, too."

"For now, let's just let him enjoy this treasure hunt."

"You know all of this happened because of the hero you made me into. The story you wrote about my involvement in helping put an end to Parker's drug activities and implicating Moody in the process got the attention of a lot important people. The reaction of public opinion wasn't bad either."

"That was only the facts, sir. You worked a long time on that thing, not to mention putting your life on the line. If Mitch thought I'd overdone the story, you can believe, I would have heard about it."

Ryan picked up a stick and began to scratch in the dirt. "At the time I agreed to take the assignment, my life seemed pretty empty. It was just after Alice died."

Stacy wished the words he spoke would dissolve in mid air. She wanted to clamp her hands over her ears. She didn't want to hear how much he loved Alice.

"I was looking for something that would require so

much from me, I wouldn't have time to think about her. I couldn't forget her, but in time, it did help numb the pain. Anyway, I want you to know I appreciate the story."

Her voice was barely audible. "You're welcome, Ryan."

He stood and rejoined the crew digging.

Chapter Seven

The sun's rays beamed down on the swamp, creating a steam bath. Stacy's clothes began to stick to her body. She shed her jacket, making her arms prime quarry for the mosquitoes. She slapped at them absent-mindedly as they buzzed around her head. Their buzzing was more annoying than their bite. Her hair had drooped and was plastered to her forehead. She found a rubber band in her jacket pocket and slicked her hair back into a ponytail.

The swamp was quiet except for the occasional scream of a hawk and the sound of the shovels as they sliced their way through the spongy damp earth. Uncle Josh had found a cypress and sat on the ground, using the tree for a backrest. Ryan squatted nearby talking quietly to him and Steve.

One of the men digging called out, "I think we've hit something. Look at this, Steve." Reaching down, the man picked up something and threw it up on the ground beside the hole. All three were on their feet in an instant and standing next to the dark hole. Steve bent down and scraped the dirt off the object with his pocketknife.

"Look's like bone to me."

"I told you so," Uncle Josh said. "Lafitte always buried a body to guard his treasure."

"More likely to dispose of wagging tongues," Ryan said. "I don't know whether it's a tibia or femur."

In his practical matter-of-fact voice Uncle Josh said, "Don't guess it matters much. That guy ain't gonna be needin' either one."

The tension of the moment was broken by laughter of the group at Uncle Josh's astute observation.

The shovel hit something that sounded loud and hollow.

"Be careful. Try to locate the outside edge of it," Steve said.

The scraping sound of the shovels made goose bumps on Stacy's arms. She hugged herself tight as she felt a rabbit run across her grave. She shivered; hoping it wasn't an omen of things to come.

"Yeah, it's a box of some kind all right," one of the men said.

Steve moved towards the truck. "I have some chain. We'll haul it up with the winch." He cranked up the engine and backed it near the hole.

Ryan jumped into the back of the truck to unwind the cable and sent it down into the hole. The two men at the bottom secured the chain around the box, attached the cable and climbed out. The motor strained loudly as the winch engaged and the box began rising. No one spoke a word as Ryan guided the rotten box to the ground.

"Hurry up, Ryan. Open her up," Uncle Josh could contain his curiosity and excitement no longer.

Ryan swung at the rust encrusted lock with a hammer. The years of water and earth had done their destructive work well. Only one swing was necessary. The lock shattered. Ryan looked up at Stacy, his eyes questioning as if she held the answer to the contents of the chest. He took a deep breath and tried to lift the lid.

Once again, the years and water held tightly onto the lid. The box refused to divulge its secrets.

Ryan picked up a crowbar and tried the second time. The bit penetrating the lid had weakened the box. It gave way, as did the side of the box. Gold doubloons, pieces of eight spilled onto the ground as well as cascades of pearls, precious gems and jewelry.

Stacy's inquisitive mind immediately raced to the need to know the kind of women who had worn these jewels. Did Lafitte kill them? Did he and his men rape them? Her mind whirled as her imagination ran away with her.

Josh ran his fingers through the gold. "Always wanted to do that ever since I saw it in the movies." His aged voice quivered with excitement. "Ryan, I want you to pick out a real purdy bauble for Stacy. We'd never found this if she hadn't brought it home to us that we were about to lose the plantation. I didn't believe it 'til I read that newspaper article she wrote. Then I thought it was already gone."

"Sure thing Uncle Josh," Ryan said as he took Stacy's hand.

Stacy was standing in back of Josh and laid her free hand on his bony old shoulder as he knelt over the pile of treasure.

"Thank you, Mr. Townsend. The story and knowing that you can keep Dawn's Promise is all I need."

Josh pulled himself to his feet and stumbled backward clutching his chest. Ryan reached for him as the old man slumped to the ground. "What's wrong, Uncle Josh?" Ryan knew the answer before he asked.

Stacy knelt and cradled his head in her lap. "Someone give me your jacket," she ordered. Steve handed his to her and she draped it over Josh's chest.

"Guess today's just been too much for this old body." His struggled to get his breath. His face twisted in pain.

"Ryan, we have to get him to a hospital." A tear

escaped down Stacy's cheek and fell on the old man's forehead.

"Naw, naw, too late. Don't y'all cry for me. Today's been one of the best days of my life. Now I'm going to be with Suzzie and tell her all about it. What could be better'n that?" He closed his eyes. His chest heaved once and he was gone.

Ryan stood dazed, disbelieving what his eyes had just witnessed. This couldn't be happening—not now.

Steve laid his hand on Ryan's shoulder. "Sorry, Ryan. He sure was excited. He died happy. Not many of us get that."

"Yeah, you're right, not many get that."

Stacy wanted to throw her arms around Ryan but she knew if she did, he would break and now was not the time.

The men lifted the old man's body and placed it in the bed of the pickup. Ryan helped Stacy into the back with Josh. She held his head in her lap for the ride back. She gently stroked the dead man's gray hair. Even though she had known him for only a short time, she had come to respect his reverence for the land, the principles he lived by and had passed on to Ryan. There were few left to whom a principle meant more than a dollar bill and Josh was one of them. He had reminded her of her own grandfather with his mischievous humor and twinkling eyes. Most of all she respected the love and care he had given Ryan.

155

The old truck carrying Josh's body and the remains of the treasure chest slowly made its way into the yard.

Annie was sitting on the porch in the rocking chair with the big Bible in her lap, rocking gently, and humming *What A Friend We Have In Jesus*.

Ryan got out of the truck and walked towards the white haired old woman.

Annie struggled to pull her stiffened body from the rocker. She wiped her eyes on her apron. "Don't have to tell me, Mista Ryan. The hounds started howling last night and been doing it off and on all morning. They always know. Y'all bring him on in. I got his dark blue suit pressed and his favorite shirt done up. Didn't like starch in his collar, so I ironed it real good."

Josh was laid to rest beside Aunt Sue in the family plot. It was a peaceful small area set under a grove of live oak trees. Josh had spent some of each day weeding or planting flowers there, but mostly talking to Sue. Now he was with her.

It had all happened so fast and with so much shock, it didn't seem real. The funeral had been a blur for Ryan. It was too much for him to comprehend—Uncle Josh gone. He went through the motions, taking care of what needed to be done. But he needed to say goodbye in his own way and alone.

The next week, Ryan stood over the grave and remembered helping Uncle Josh keep the little cemetery neat when he was a boy. It was always a special time for them both. He wasn't unhappy with Josh's passing. It was time. The world was getting too complicated for the straightforward thinking old man. Josh's philosophy of life was that right was right, wrong was wrong, and never the twain would meet— no matter how much rationalization went on. He was convinced that the gray area that the law now tolerated, that parents tolerated, that even society tolerated would destroy his America.

As Ryan's worldly knowledge loomed in law school and his arguing skills became honed, he and Uncle Josh had entered into many heated debates on such perplexities. No matter how intelligently and logically Ryan played devils advocate, he knew the old man was right. He would miss their good-natured arguments and getting levelheaded advice whether he asked for it or not.

"See you later, Uncle Josh." Ryan turned and slowly strolled back to the car. Stacy would be expecting him.

As he drove into New Orleans, he thought of her. She was so different from the facade she portrayed. She always appeared so perfect. She looked as if she would melt like cotton candy at the first hint of trouble. But she had proven she didn't run from anything. He couldn't get the picture of her out of his head, on the night of the drug bust. How calm she'd been. How professionally she'd done her job. He knew that if he had been mixed up with Parker, she would have severed their relationship in a minute. She had said as much. He knew she thrived on the adrenaline that pulsed through her body that night and the recognition she had received from writing the story. Would she be willing to give that up?

He could still see her face glow and eyes shine as the chest was opened. She had been thrilled for him and Uncle Josh. And then the devastation that had shown with a hint of a tear in her eye as Uncle Josh lay in her lap. She was the kind of woman that wouldn't buckle regardless of what came. She was the wife he wanted.

Dealers and collectors were on the phone as soon as Stacy's headline hit the street and Ryan had no trouble turning the treasure into cash. It had been valued at five and a half million dollars and everyone thought they had to own something with the Lafitte name connected to it.

He donated two of the items to the Louisiana State Museum at Jackson Square. An eight inch long cross encrusted with diamonds, emeralds and rubies along with the gold chain that went with it and a tiara, covered with gems that a queen could have worn. He could think of no more perfect place for them. Josh would have approved, he was sure.

He had been fortunate. According to Louisiana law, half of discovered antiquities go to the finder and half to the owner of the land. Ryan was the finder because he had hired Steve and his seismic company. He'd paid all costs and given Steve and his crew a generous bonus. The men had been elated. And he had inherited the plantation from Uncle Josh, making him the property owner; therefore, he became owner of the whole treasure.

After news of the drug bust, he became a celebrity around New Orleans. People stopped to shake his hand. There was no problem getting a last minute reservation at the best restaurants.

The position waiting on him in the attorneys general's office would pave the way for politics and that was what Ryan had always had his eye on. Uncle Josh had felt strongly about some changes that needed to be made. Maybe he could bring them about. This would be a way he could give back some of what he owed the old man who had shared so much with him. If Stacy would say yes tonight, he would have all any man could ask.

He only hoped he would live long enough to enjoy his future with her. The threat of Quesada and his thugs gnawed at his brain. It always would until they were put where they belonged, but he couldn't live his life in fear. That wouldn't be living at all.

Chapter Eight

Stacy looked forward to seeing the production of *Arsenic and Old Lace*. This would be the first evening out since Josh's death and the finding of the treasure. She knew they needed a respite from the turmoil in their lives these last few weeks.

She chose a yellow strapless pique dress and short jacket for the occasion. As she dressed, her thoughts were of Uncle Josh. Not only had she respected the old man, she had loved his sense of devilment and humor. It was as if she and Josh shared a secret. The secret being that she loved Ryan from the first meeting. She hadn't recognized it, but Josh had. She thought Ryan was handling the loss of his uncle well. Still, it was sad that such an exciting and joyous time for both of them had to end so tragically.

Stacy had written a retraction of the auction, the story of the discovery of the treasure, the history of the Townsend family and Josh's obituary in the same article. While the outcome had been sad, the story was captivating. Mitch had been so excited reading it, he couldn't keep still in his leather chair. Stacy had to smile watching him. She had hit pay dirt herself.

The state hummed with excitement. Again her story was the headliner. Her career was going well and she thrived on the stimulus. She could think of nothing that she wanted more at this moment than the success she was experiencing.

When Stacy opened the door, Ryan beamed broadly at the sight of her. He picked her up and swung her petite body around the room.

"Ryan Townsend, put me down. I've worked all evening to get this dress just right and you'll destroy me in five minutes."

"You'd be the best looking woman there even in a flour sack—and probably more fun." He had that sly slant to his smile that made him look like an impertinent rake. Stacy blushed. He laughed out loud at her.

"We're going to be late. Curtain goes up at eight," she said.

"I've got reservations after the play at Commander's Palace. Is that all right with you?" he asked.

"You know that's my favorite."

"Yeah, and I know why—that white chocolate mousse with raspberry sauce," he teased.

"Well, I haven't seen you leave a crumb of garlic bread in the basket either," she snapped back.

We're acting like old married people already, he thought.

They enjoyed the play, in spite of feeling as if they were the ones on stage. Everyone seemed to want to congratulate Ryan on finding the treasure or give condolences over the death of Uncle Josh. Several just wanted to be introduced to the woman on his arm. It was obvious that a lot of the women were aware of Ryan's being an eligible bachelor. His stock had gone up significantly since he'd become wealthy, Stacy thought. She smiled sweetly while secretly wanting to scratch their eyes out. Maybe his eyes would be the better idea. Her thoughts ran on. He does enjoy the attention.

They received the same welcome at the restaurant. The maître d' escorted them to a table in the center of the room. "We are so glad to see you and your charming companion, Mr. Townsend. May I congratulate on your discovery?" The maître d' made a flourish in the air with his hand.

"It's been the talk of the restaurant the last two weeks. Everyone was just so intoxicated with news."

Ryan smiled at the effeminate gesture. "Thank

you, Allen. It was exciting for a while. What looks good tonight?"

"Ahh, the snapper is wonderful as well as the rack of lamb. May I suggest that you start with the Oysters a la Marinie're? Shall I send the wine steward?"

"Yes, please." Ryan looked over and smiled at Stacy. "We're definitely celebrating tonight. Tonight it will be Dom Perignon."

"Ryan, that's too expensive. I'd be just as happy with the Vouvray we usually get," Stacy said.

"No, that won't do for tonight."

Enjoying their meal was difficult with so many eyes watching every move they made. Stacy took her first sip of Dom Perignon and decided that, yes, she would be just as happy with the Vouvray. She thought that Ryan was acting strange this evening. Pleasant enough, but strange. She wondered if it had anything to do with all the attention that he had been receiving recently. How long would it last?

She didn't ask him any questions of importance during the meal. They had both already learned how much is overheard in even the noisiest of restaurants. They finished their dinner, said their goodnights around the restaurant and left.

It was one of those still balmy Louisiana evenings. The moon was only half full and the black sky sparkled with stars. Stacy drew in a deep breath of the cool damp air. It would be a clear night for the southern city. Fall would soon be moving in. Leaves would be turning.

"Feels good to be out in the air," she said.

"Yeah, they always have such a crowd, sometimes it gets a little close. Let's drive out to the lake. It should be a nice out there," Ryan said.

Stacy turned on the radio. Julio Iglesias crooned out his *Starry Night* album.

"We'll soon have a CD player, in the new car. I've decided that this old Chevy is about ready to be put out to pasture. What make do you want," he asked?

"It's your car and I'm happy with the radio," she answered.

He pulled onto the sandy shore of the lake and cut the engine. "Want to walk?" he asked.

"I have heels and hose on."

"Take them off."

He got out and walked down to the water's edge. Stacy removed her shoes and hose. The sand crunched between her toes. So much for my polish she thought. The sand was wet close to the lake's edge and a slight chill caused her to shiver. Ryan had removed his socks and shoes and rolled his pants cuffs up. He had tucked something under his arm she hadn't noticed before—a blanket. She felt a little nervous. They weren't kids and it was a little late for blanket parties. He'd always been a gentleman, even if not perfect. What did he have in mind?

The radio played low in the background. He spread the blanket on the ground, sat down on it and gave her skirt a tug. Losing her balance, she sat down clumsily. The momentum of the action pulled her over and she found herself lying on her side. He was on top of her in an instant.

"Got you now, my lovely," he hissed in a sinister Simon Legree voice and planted his lips over hers firmly. It startled her. The dream, Lafitte, and the kidnapping flooded back into her consciousness. She felt frightened.

The weight of Ryan's body hampered her breathing. Panic set in. She thrashed wildly at him. "Ryan, get off me." Gasping for breath, she struggled against his broad chest. She couldn't budge him. He didn't look as strong as he was. He slid his body off to the side, but continued to kiss her until her body relaxed.

"You're safe, Stac. I'll never harm you."

The quietness of his voice calmed her. Fear left her body and the mantle of quiet submission covered her. She did feel safe—and cherished. She had wondered what love would feel like when it came along. Now she knew.

"Stacy, I have to ask you something." He pulled her to a sitting position, reached into his pocket and pulled out a velvet ring box.

For a moment, Stacy thought her heart had ceased beating.

"The night of the drug bust, I realized that I never want you in danger again, Stacy. I want to protect and take care of you for the rest of my life. I want you to be my wife. Marry me, Stacy."

Stacy's head swam. This wasn't the proposal she had dreamed of. All he could see was what he wanted. Would this be what marriage was like with him? He hadn't mentioned love at all. She felt ice crystals forming over her heart.

A choked, desperate laugh escaped her lips. "Ryan, reporting is my profession and sometimes, danger goes with the territory."

"I know. That's why I've decided you're going to quit the paper."

"Quit the paper?" Her ears rang with disbelief. He had already made the decision for her.

"Stacy, I'm wealthy now. You don't need to work. You can have anything you want. I'll take care of you." He had stopped just short of adding "little lady."

Stacy began to quiver and clenched her fists to contain the explosion she felt building.

Slowly, he opened the box.

Stacy peered down at the biggest, most ostentatious diamond she had ever seen. And this one, she had seen before. She sucked in her breath at its beauty and seethed with anger at the same time.

"Ryan, I don't need you to take care of me. I've been taking care of myself since I was a kid. I need your love and understanding." She searched his eyes for some sign of acknowledgment of what she was saying. "Ryan, I need to be a partner in our marriage."

Ryan hadn't heard her at all. He was wrapped in the excitement of the moment and simply continued with his planned proposal.

"Uncle Josh told me to give you a bauble. Thought you might like this one from both of us."

He wasn't listening. A voice deep from where a woman's intuition lives whispered that if he wasn't listening now—he never would.

"The most dangerous thing I want my wife doing is driving the kids to school. Stacy, all you'll have to do is run my home and take care of my children."

She could conceal her anger and disappointment no longer. Manicured nails dug into her palms.

"I didn't know you had any children." She spat out the words and forced a shallow laugh.

"You know what I mean, when we have children."

My wife, my home, my children—the words boiled in her brain. Her humiliation and pain had turned to fury. He hadn't used the word "our" once.

The tone made her a possession. His self-centered domineering nature had shown itself. Why hadn't she seen it before? There was no way she could be happy with this man. He had no comprehension that a marriage was two individuals working together—and that meant equality. She would settle for nothing less. She couldn't.

"Ryan, I won't give up my career. You have no idea of the sacrifices I've made. I've worked too hard to get through school and get my career where it is now. I need it." She searched his face for understanding.

Ryan stared blankly at her not comprehending what was happening.

"Don't you see? I wouldn't be the girl you love without it and Ryan; I'm good at it. No, I certainly don't need you to take care of me."

Stacy's chest felt so tight that she thought it would burst. "You want to put me on a shelf so I can watch life pass me by and take me down when you deem and I'm supposed to be happy with that?" She didn't realize her voice was booming. "Ryan, I need a man who will love me for who I am and that means a man who will accept my profession. Which I might add, is as valuable to me as yours is to you." She placed her hands on her hips and boldly met his eyes. "I'm sorry. There's no way in hell you're going to run my life like that. No, Ryan, I won't accept your ring or your pompous attitude."

Ryan's eyes glazed over. "I see." He snapped the box shut. "Uncle Josh said give it to you. There it is." He flipped it over into her lap.

Stacy inhaled a deep breath and grappled with regaining her composure. She lifted the ring box from her lap and folded his hand over it and said softly, "Ryan, it's a beautiful ring and someday the girl will come along who can wear it. But, it's not me." Hot tears rolled down her cheeks as she got to her feet, turned her back and walked slowly to the car. She had wanted to be his wife more than he would ever know but not like this. She couldn't.

Ryan snatched up the sandy blanket, shook it once with a loud pop and stomped off toward the car grinding his toes into the sand with every step.

The drive back into town was frozen in tension and silence. When they reached her apartment, Stacy opened her car door and tested the depth of his anger. "Will I see you this week?"

"I'm going to be in Baton Rouge this week working on *my* career. Since it means so much to you, maybe you'd better do the same." He jerked the door shut with a slam and sped off down the street. Stacy could hear his tires squeal as he turned the corner.

Spoiled little boy. He always got his way with Aunt Sue and Uncle Josh. Under her breath she said, "I don't need a lifetime of that. Thank you very much." Through blurry eyes, she fumbled to open the door to the lobby. The night guard gave her a confused look as she entered shoes in hand. She was glad he didn't say anything. Her eyes stared straight ahead as she struggled to keep the tears from flowing.

Ryan stared into the darkness of the night. He wanted to lash out at the world, but for now, the car would have to take the abuse. He smashed the acceler-ator to the floor. The car responded with a roar and shot forward.

He couldn't understand what had happened. Was it so criminal to want to protect and provide for her? What had he said? He hadn't prepared himself for this. It had taken all his strength to put Alice's death behind him and dare to hope that love would ever come along again. The largest hurdle of his life had been regaining the trust that love wouldn't be jerked from him the sec-ond time. And now—Stacy's rejection. Anger welled in him and he slammed his fist into the steering wheel. It wasn't fair.

Annie had stayed on at Dawn's Promise. It was the only home she had ever known, but it was becoming increasing difficult for her. With Josh gone, there just wasn't as much to occupy her time. She missed his banging and puttering around the house. Meal times were the worse. She and Josh had sat at the same table for years, enjoying their meals, discussing the world situation, remarking on how times had changed and what would become of them. The quiet was almost too much to bear. Also, Annie was getting up in years. She was almost the same age as Josh and keeping up with the cleaning, climbing the stairs and cooking was

a big job. Finally, she recognized that she needed people to do for and those 'Little Heathen' as she affectionately called her grandchildren, needed her firm
hand of guidance.

Marcy, Annie's daughter, drove from Houston to
take Annie back with her. Both she and her mother
agreed that Annie could do with a "little vacation."
Marcy was sure that Annie wouldn't be coming back to
Dawn's Promise, but for now, it was just a little vacation. They could get the rest of her things as she wanted them. Annie would come to terms with the reality
of the situation in her own time.

Ryan drove out to the plantation to see her off. She
and Marcy were putting the last of her luggage in the
Ford wagon as he pulled up. He approached the old
woman, put his arms around her and gave her a big
hug. Annie had been such a large part of his growing
up. Dawn's Promise wouldn't be same without her.
He took her purse out of her hands, snapped it open and
placed a folded cashiers check for one hundred thousand dollars in it and handed it back to her.

"That doesn't begin to repay what Uncle Josh and
I owe you, Annie, but maybe it will make things a little easier. You were real good to Uncle Josh, Annie. I
never worried about him as long as you were in charge
here. I want to thank you for that."

"Yeh sir. Thank ya, Mr. Ryan. Me and Mr. Josh
been good friends since we wuz younguns." She

laughed. "One time, when my Mama was cook for the big house, I'd stay wif her in the kitchen. I was bout five then. I wanted some sweet so I stole a piece of apple pie of what was left over from supper. Mama started to serve that pie the next evening and there wasn't enough. She pitched a fit. I was going to get my britches busted for sho. Then Mr. Josh, they called him Joshie then, well, he come in the kitchen and see what's happening. He told her he took the pie. She knowed he didn't, but she didn't give me a whippen neither. Since that day, me and Mr. Josh always watch out for each other."

Ryan laughed at the old woman. "You two must have been the terror of the place growing up."

"Yeh Sir, I specks we wuz. Now, Mr. Ryan, when you need me, you call. I'll be right back here."

"Annie, right now, I don't know what I'll do. I'd like to restore the plantation to the way it was but that seems rather senseless just for myself."

"Mista Ryan, you like one of my own kids and I'll tell you this much. Miss Stacy might not knowed it, but she got it bad for you and she belongs here. Did you see that chil's eyes the first day she walked through this house?"

"Annie, liking a house and being a wife is two different things. Stacy has a career and she's not willing to give it up to become Mrs. Ryan Townsend or Mistress of Dawn's Promise."

"Why should she? Are you gonna give up being a lawyer just cause you marry and inherit this place? No, you ain't, and you've got no call to 'spect her to give up what she worked so hard for." Annie shook her head. "I ain't had a man for a lot of years now, Mr. Ryan, but I ain't forgot what makes a good marriage. *Fairness.* That's the whole thing. Ya can put up with a awful lot ifn ya fair with each other." The old black woman's wisdom put a red-hot poker through his heart.

Marcy turned her eyes away from the conversation to avoid seeing Ryan's embarrassment. Her mother had always had a knack of putting things in their simplest terms. She had experienced the brunt of it many times. Just now, Annie had put Ryan just where she wanted him and he was feeling more than a little uncomfortable with the truth. He helped Annie into the car.

"Marcy, if she needs anything, you have my number."

"Yes, I do and thank you, Mr. Townsend." Marcy said. She started the car and drove off. The old woman waved out of the window as her old eyes took their last look at home.

Chapter Nine

The next morning, Stacy waited for Mitch to come into the office. She scarcely let him settle with the usual morning cup of coffee before she knocked on the door.

"Come in." He glanced at her. "Hey, Stac, what's up?"

"Mitch, I need to talk to you when it's convenient."

"I've got time now. Come on in." Mitch could tell by the expression on Stacy's face that something was terribly wrong. "Huh-oh. What's bothering you? Anything I can do?"

"No, I suppose when you think about it, everything is right—except me." She paused and took a deep breath before continuing. "Ryan asked me to marry him."

"That's great. I'm happy for you both."

"You don't understand, Mitch, I can't marry him. I've worked too hard to give up my career. I love what I do and he expects a full time wife. He's demanding that I quit the paper. The problem is at a standoff, I'm afraid."

"I see. Well, I damn sure don't want to lose a reporter with your talent and tenacity, Stacy. But I understand Ryan's point of view too, especially if he's headed where I think he is. It would be difficult for the public to understand why the wife of the Attorney General of Louisiana works."

Angrily Stacy snapped back, "Yeah, heaven forbid that she might want to make something of her life also. Even more of a crime that she has a brain. That's just too much for the public to deal with in bayou country." Stacy's eyes blazed. Her voice rose to a high-pitch. "These parishes haven't even gotten accustomed to the idea that women are going on the pill and taking control of their own bodies yet."

Mitch grinned holding his hands up in surrender. "Whoa, I'm on your side."

"I'm sorry, I'm just not myself today. I didn't mean to take it out on you, Mitch."

"Well, Stac, let's look at this from a different angle. If you're planning on going into politics it couldn't hurt to have a good paper behind you. A talented wife that reports for that paper and knows just how to present

your side of the issues, could be nothing but an asset."
He brushed his hand over the stray lock of hair. "Not
that I wouldn't back him anyway, you understand, but
you would still be a great help in his corner. I've
known Ryan a long time and I think his views are just
what this state needs." Mitch looked up at her with the
boyish grin on his face. "But he doesn't have to know
that just yet."

"No," Stacy said. "I wouldn't even want the issue
of how I could help him to be considered. Anyway, the
point is that I need to get away from the whole thing for
a while. I'll be fine, I just need some time."

"I've been wanting to talk to you about something
anyway. Maybe this is the time." Stacy sat down to
listen to Mitch. "After the treasure was found, there
was a lot of interest in that story about Lafitte. I
thought it might not be a bad idea to do a follow up,"
he said.

"Yes, that's a good idea. I really got interested in
Lafitte. Maybe, I could do a story on the man, as
opposed to hero or scoundrel."

"Yeah, let's see if we can give the history aspect a
little different twist. It won't be a first pager, but it
would make a great Sunday special and give you the
time you want."

"Thanks, Mitch. I'll get right on it." She stood and
turned to go.

"Stac, keep in touch just in case something pops

here and I need you." What he didn't say was so I can keep Ryan informed of your whereabouts when he comes to his senses.

"I will and thanks again. I won't forget it." Stacy spent the next day in the Williams Research Center on Chartres Street. She read journals that were supposedly written by Jean Lafitte and accounts of him written by others. Friday afternoon she called Mitch.

"Mitch, I'm going to Galveston to do more investigation."

"How's it going, Stac?" he asked. "Have you heard anything from Ryan?"

The question jabbed at Stacy's heart. She didn't want to discuss Ryan. The wounds were still too fresh and too deep. She avoided the issue. "The research is going well. You can almost sympathize with Lafitte in some areas. Did you know he saw his child butchered when they were driven out of the Louisiana swamp?"

Mitch had heard the quick intake of Stacy's breath when he mentioned Ryan and sensed she was avoiding the question. He wished he hadn't asked. "Knew he had a reputation of being a ladies man, but I didn't know he was a father."

"According to my research, Lafitte married a Houma Indian by the name of Marie. Together they, supposedly, named the bayous of Terrebonne Parish.

As to the human side, I found an account of him secretly feeding biscuits to a sailor dying of a stomach tumor. His ship had been stranded in the Sabine swamp by a fallen cypress tree. Food supplies were scarce. If his men had discovered he was wasting food on the expiring man, it would probably cost him his life." She continued without hesitating. "His men even dismembered, cooked and ate the corpse. According to the journal, he didn't take part. It's a gruesome tale but who knows if it's true or not."

"Good Lord, Stacy."

"Anyway, he served in 1819 as governor of a commune called Campeche. That's now Galveston. So I thought I'd take off down there and see what I could come up with."

"Sounds like you've dug up some interesting information. I'm anxious to see it." He paused a moment fully aware that Stacy was still evading the important question. "Stacy, take care of yourself."

Stacy knew Mitch was concerned about her. She owed him some sort of an answer. "Mitch, as to the other question, no, I haven't heard from Ryan. He said he had some business in Baton Rouge. As angry as he was, I doubt if I will."

"He'll come around, Stacy."

"I don't expect it to go any farther, Mitch, but I would like to remain friends. I truly hope he finds someone who can be what he needs." Her voice cracked. "I'll call you later. Bye," she said, and hurriedly replaced the receiver. Stacy lowered her head, resting it on the back of her forearm. Tears and tension flowed freely. "Ryan, Ryan, I do love you so."

She returned to New Orleans Thursday afternoon and went straight to the office.

"Glad to see you back, Stacy." Mitch rose to put his arm around her shoulder. He had become the big brother she had always wanted.

"I'm fine, Mitch, I told you I would be."

"Got something I want to show you." He opened the afternoon edition to page eight. A small picture of Ryan appeared in the left corner. The title read, *Ryan Townsend, Recent Discoverer of Lafitte's Treasure to Dedicate Park in Memory of his Uncle, Mr. Josiah Townsend.* The dedication was scheduled for October the thirteenth, Uncle Josh's birthday.

"I think you should cover it, Stacy."

"Mitch, it would be too uncomfortable for both of us."

"You don't get it. You're not going alone. Danielle's already in on this and she thinks it's a great idea."

"What have you got in mind?" she asked suspiciously.

"Bringing Mr. Townsend to his senses and in a hurry. Danielle told a few of her closest friends that she and I have broken up. If I know these friends, it was all over New Orleans in fifteen minutes."

"I don't understand. How's that going to change

anything?"

"Danielle will be expected to be at that dedication, so she gets one her friends to take her. I'm taking you and we're going to lay it on thick for Mr. Townsend. If he's anything like he was in high school, he won't be able to stand it."

"You mean, make him jealous. Mitch, I don't want to do that. I could have had him if I were willing to give up—myself. I'm still not willing to do that."

"I don't think you'll have to. Listen Stac, what have you got to lose by trying? Are you going to be kicking yourself twenty years from now if you don't?" He pushed the ever-present lock of hair out of his face and his eyes snapped with glee and mischief.

"Mr. McGalliard, you're a devil."

"Well," he drawled out. "I owe Ryan one, but that's another story."

Jackson Square was the hubbub of excitement and chatter. It looked as if all of New Orleans had turned out for the dedication. Every member of the New Orleans Historical Society must have shown up. Each of the women members seemed to be trying to outdo the other with her new fall ensemble. Sugar coated southern voices greeted each other with, "Hello, Darling, how have you been?" and "Yes, we were in Provence this summer."

Mitch affectionately called the group The

"Hysterical" Society. The gentlemen were engaged in trying for one-upmanship for the politician's favors and paving the way for the next business transaction. The fact remained that they were one of the more influential groups in New Orleans. If politics was your game, you needed them and that was the game for Ryan Townsend.

Governor Rice and his beautiful, dark-haired Cajun wife had taken their place of honor on the stage. They waved to different people they recognized in the crowd. Occasionally, they would engage in conversation with one or the other guests on the floor. No doubt these were large contributors of campaign money.

The band from Tulane blared out a Sousa march. Mitch held on to Stacy's arm protectively as they made their way to the front section that had been roped off for dignitaries and honored guests.

Stacy had chosen a navy blue suit with a yellow spun silk turtleneck for the occasion. Her look was tailored but not stiff. She knew the dash of yellow would set off her dark hair and eyes. Ryan liked her in yellow.

"You look stunning, Stac. Just relax and follow my lead," Mitch said.

Danielle and a young good-looking blond haired man approached the area of seated dignitaries. "Who's that with Danielle?" Stacy whispered. The young man had a rakish look about him and a body that Tarzan would have envied. Mitch looked down at his freshly shined shoes and slid his hand across his mouth to keep from laughing out loud.

"That's Bobby Tipton, her personal trainer," he said. "She must have waited until the last minute to ask someone." He caught Danielle's eye and they both smiled secretively at each other, then quickly redirected their attentions to their companions. Mitch thought Bobby was enjoying his assignment a little too much but he understood from different sources that Tipton cared more for boys than girls. That was probably why Danielle had asked him. Mitch placed his arm around Stacy's shoulders and whispered in her ear. She smiled affectionately at him just in case Ryan had already located them in the crowd. If she was going to be party to this charade, she might as well do a good job of it.

The band concluded their number with an abrupt halt. The mayor stepped to the podium to begin what promised to be long boring introductions. Attorney General Anderson gave a speech recapping the discovery of the treasure and what it meant to the state. More importantly, he praised the work Ryan had done in seeing that a drug ring had been closed in New Orleans. He introduced Ryan and the crowd rose to its feet in applause.

Mitch frowned and looked around at the crowd.

"What's wrong, Mitch?" Stacy asked.

"This would be a perfect time for one of Quesada's

men to pick him off. He's a perfect target up on that stage."

"Oh God, Mitch."

"Wait a minute. Look up, Stacy."

The roofs of the surrounding buildings were covered with uniformed men brandishing rifles. "They'd get a sniper in the blink of an eye, Stac." Mitch grinned. "Looks like the Attorney General is taking good care of his boy."

Stacy breathed a sigh of relief.

Ryan's dark eyes locked onto Stacy's the minute he began his speech. He gave a brief history of the Townsend family and told the audience what kind of man Josh had been, what he had believed, and of the love he had held for his home state of Louisiana. He then made the dedication in the name of Josh Townsend. The Governor concluded with the acceptance of the gracious gift of four hundred acres of the marsh land and swamp area to be used for a Jean Lafitte National Historical Park and Preserve.

Stacy sat quietly, kneading her fingers in her lap. She remembered the first day that she'd met Josh. The gravelly words of the old man, expressing his feelings and views of the government ending up with his land, still rang in her ears. Now she thought he would approve.

This would help Ryan on his way up the political ladder. The philanthropic gesture would assure his acceptance in circles that could help him to the Governor's Mansion. Even though she had never heard him say that's what he wanted, she knew it was. Yes, she was sure that Josh was dancing a jig. He would have helped Ryan anyway he could. The band played *You Are My Sunshine*. Ryan gazed steadily at Stacy.

People moved forward to shake Ryan's hand. He strained over the crowd to keep Stacy in view.

Stacy made a move in the direction of the stage to join the procession. Mitch abruptly stopped her by placing a hand on her shoulder.

"Uh-uh, there's a private reception at Commanders Palace. We'll do our congratulating there. Let's just let him simmer a bit."

Live oaks lined the street in front of the turquoise and white restaurant. As guests arrived, the jazz band played *When the Saints Come Marching In*. Mitch purposefully made a late arrival so he and Stacy would make an entrance. Taking Stacy's hand, he led her through the maze of people and up the stairs to the Garden Room. The room, done in white latticework, mirrors, and glass, overlooked a three-hundred-year-old live oak. The garden below was in full bloom. The setting couldn't have been more perfect.

As Mitch and Stacy moved through the crowd, Mitch made a point to introduce Stacy as his "friend."

He was careful to give her a squeeze or adoring look as he did it. Stacy thought he was hamming it up a little too much, but he was having such a good time, she went along with it.

A large group congregated near the middle of the room. Mitch was sure Ryan was the center of attention. Danielle was involved in conversation with him at the moment. The band broke into a slow dance tempo and the two stepped onto the dance floor. Mitch followed and swung Stacy out onto the floor, nuzzling his face into her hair. It smelled like gardenias. He hoped Ryan had observed the nuzzling gesture.

Ryan was engaged in conversation but hadn't missed anything Mitch and Stacy had done since they entered the room.

"Danielle, what happened between you and Mitch? I thought you two were about ready to right a long overdue wrong," Ryan said.

"So did I," she said. "Mitch decided he needed more time. He didn't come right and say so but I know he's seeing quite a lot of Stacy. Oh, there they are." Danielle wanted to make sure that Ryan saw them and the show Mitch was putting on. "You can't blame him, I suppose. She is a beautiful and an extremely smart lady," Danielle purred.

"Well, you're not chopped liver in that department either," he said.

Danielle smiled. "Thanks for saying so, Ryan.

Danielle looked far away. "Stacy doesn't seem to back up from anything and I know that adventurous spirit is a real turn on for Mitch. I have to face the fact, they make a good team."

Ryan was quiet. Danielle placed her head on his shoulder in fear that if he looked at her, the laugh that was bubbling up in her throat would escape. She deserved an academy award, which she fully intended to claim from Mitch.

Danielle made eye contact with Mitch over Ryan's shoulder. She winked. Mitch smiled back. Taking the cue, he guided Stacy toward them.

"Hello Ryan, that was a fine speech. I sure wish Josh could have heard it," Mitch said, sticking out his hand.

Ryan took it. "Thanks, Mitch." He was speaking to Mitch, but those dark eyes were riveted on Stacy.

"Hello, Stacy, how have you been?"

"Fine. Awfully busy at the paper. And you?"

"Yeah, we've been busy," Mitch echoed, as he gave Stacy's hair a single stroke. Danielle glared at him. Her eyes told him he was enjoying the acting much too much. He caught the accusation in her look, lowered his arm, placing it around Stacy's waist and danced her off in another direction.

Ryan spoke up as the couple drifted off.

"Stacy, save me a dance later." Mitch had his back to Ryan. Glancing down at Stacy, he grinned from ear to ear as if to say, "Told you so." Stacy quickly looked away from him and back to Ryan.

"Yes, of course, Mr. Townsend." She laid her head on Mitch's chest in a loving gesture so Ryan couldn't see her face. The smile found its way to her mouth and teetered close to a full-blown giggle. Mitch danced her off the floor and out of Ryan's sight before they both collapsed into laughter.

"You're giving me a scalding bad reputation, Miss Stimmons. They all think we're drunk." They broke into another round of snickering. Regaining composure took some effort. Mitch remembered how long it had been since lunch.

"I'm hungry, Stac, let's get something to eat." She nodded and they strolled toward the hors d'oeuvres table. She placed two stuffed fan-tailed shrimp, a crab-meat crepe and two oysters Rockefeller on her plate and asked for a glass of Chardonnay. Looking back over her shoulder, Mitch was still piling on the scrumptious offerings.

He joined her at a small table overlooking the dance floor. Mitch looked around, trying to locate Danielle. Bobby Tipton had replaced Ryan. He twirled her around the dance floor with some proficiency. She had removed the jacket to her emerald green dress, converting it to a cocktail look. With her creamy skin and auburn hair, it was a stunning sight. Mitch's eyes softened with adoration as he thought,

God, she's a beautiful woman and I love her. Always have. Always will.

Stacy read his mind. "She is beautiful, isn't she? I really owe her for tonight. I know you two would like to be together."

"If I know Danielle, she's the one who's had the most fun and yes, she's gorgeous. So was her mother from what I hear." The look in Stacy's eyes indicated that she wanted to know more. "Her name was Cathleen McMahon from Ireland and was the talk of New Orleans. Same stunning coloring as Danielle and not bashful. She reigned as Mardi Gras Queen and over Alexander Derusseau all his life. He worshipped the ground she walked on. Never married after her. . . ." Mitch's story was cut short.

"Stacy, may I have this dance?" Ryan laid his hand on Mitch's shoulder. "You don't mind, do you, Mitch?"

"No, of course not. Just bring her back in the same condition you found her."

Stacy felt like an old jalopy they had probably traded back and forth in high school. She held her tongue and moved onto the dance floor with Ryan.

"I've missed you, Stacy." He pulled her closer to him.

Her pulse raced and she hoped it didn't show. "You knew my phone number. I haven't heard from you in three weeks. Did you expect me to go into mourning?"

"No, I needed some time. I told you that, Stacy."

"Ryan, time is what life is made of and I only have one of those. I intend to make every minute of it count. What you do with yours is up to you."

"What's going on with you and Mitch?"

"I really don't think that's any of your concern."

"Damn it, Stac. You know you don't love him. You're only using him to get back at me. I never would have thought he would give up Danielle after waiting for her so long. You don't know what you've done to her."

"Done to her? She's the one that went off and married Roland Parker didn't she? I think you've got it backwards. She did it to Mitch. She's getting just what she deserves." Even though it was an act, Stacy's conscience cringed because she was saying such things about Danielle. Danielle was a true friend.

"You're not going to marry Mitch. I won't let you."

Stacy's temper flared. "You won't let me? I don't know what you think you can do about it."

"Stacy, you love me. You know you do. Marry me."

Stacy stopped dancing and stepped away from him. "You don't want me. You want a perfect little wife who will smile sweetly to people she can't stand just to get you elected to office." She propped her hands on hips. "Someone who will act as if she hasn't got a brain in her head and be contented to stay home and make cookies."

Ryan shook his head not believing the scene she was making.

"That's not me. Ryan, we've been over this and my feelings haven't changed. You'd grow to hate the exact thing you want me to be and if you weren't so dense, you'd see this."

Couples stopped dancing and watched the disruption. Ryan glared at her, clenching his jaw and tightly curled in his fingers to make a fist at his sides. Turning sharply on his heel, he left her standing on the dance floor alone. Stacy watched him stride away. Her face stung with fiery anger and embarrassment. Her shoulders shuddered with tension. Mitch was to her rescue immediately. Mitch was always there when she needed him. Danielle was a lucky girl.

"That didn't look as if it went well."

"It didn't. Can we go, Mitch?"

"Sure." Mitch took her by the hand and led her to the car. Why wasn't she crying? Most females Mitch knew would have been in hysterics. He wished she was. Her quietness bothered him more.

They arrived at her apartment and Mitch walked her to the door.

"Chin up, Stacy. We haven't lost the battle yet."

"Mitch, it's over. Please, just let it be."

"Are you sure that's the way you want it?"

"It's not the way I want it but it's the way it is. I need to accept that and move on."

Mitch placed a kiss on her forehead.

"You need to go. Danielle will be expecting you. Tell her how much I appreciate what she did for me. I won't forget it."

"I'll tell her. See you tomorrow. Good night, Stacy."

Once inside the door and surrounded with the coziness and safety of her home, the tension of the disastrous evening began to subside. She made herself a cup of tea and sat down at her little kitchen table with a yellow legal pad and pen. She could hear her granny say, "Write it down, Honey. It won't look like such a big problem when you get a good look at it." The practice of solving difficulties in this manner had stayed with her from childhood. She reached for the pen. She listed what she had to work with and decided not to dwell on what she didn't. Anything to get her mind off the calamity the evening had turned into. She made lists of goals and plans for accomplishing them. She scribbled up two pages of the yellow paper with new hobbies to learn, new sports to get involved in, and a list of phone numbers of organizations to join to make new friends.

Without warning she snatched up the tablet, threw it across the kitchen and burst into tears. Who was she kidding? Other than career, what did she want? She wanted Ryan Townsend to love her enough to learn to compromise. She wanted Dawn's Promise to be home and she wanted Ryan's babies to grow up there as he had. She wanted Ryan to be happy. This came as a shock to her after the way he had acted. It was the first time in her life someone else's happiness was more important that her own. She wanted Ryan to feel the same way about her.

Chapter Ten

The sun was setting as Stacy stepped from the office and made her way towards her car. Wind gusted across the parking lot, blowing grit into her eyes and hair. She pushed the stray wisp out of her face and blinked to clear her eyes of the stinging sand. She felt grimy. This week her spirits hadn't up to her usually sunny disposition. She knew why, but didn't want to admit it—even to herself. It would be another evening with a Lean Cuisine and the television set. A couple of the girls from the office had attempted to cheer her up by inviting her for dinner and drinks. Stacy turned down the invitation. She'd only put a damper on their evening and sitting in a bar with the girls had never been her idea of a good time.

Maybe she'd stop off at the health club to work off some tension and frustration. Exercise usually helped when she felt a little down, but this wasn't a "little" down. She had no way of knowing how long this black cloud would hover but until it lifted, she would rather be alone. Other women had lost the love of their life and survived. So would she.

Her career would be the most important course in her life. She mustn't let anything divert her from it. Work was the best thing for her and the more grueling, the better. She often got wrapped up in a story and would lose all sense of time. Something shocking and different was always happening in New Orleans. There would be no scarcity of something to write about. It would be a never-ending learning experience that kept boredom at bay for a lifetime, if necessary. It seemed to have worked for Mitch. Maybe it would for her.

The trial came at the end of the day when the sun retreated and darkness arrived; then depression washed over her, sucking the energy from her body and leaving her feeling hollow and insignificant.

The wind plastered her skirt against her legs as she walked. Stacy tugged at the restriction attempting to free them. Turning her back to the wind she rummaged through her bag looking for the keys to her Grand Am. She fished them out and poked a key into the lock.

Screeching tires shattered her concentration. A black Lincoln sedan bore down on her. She jumped as close to her car as she could to avoid being hit. The brakes screamed as it halted beside her. Two men dressed in dark suits jumped from the back seat of the car. One went to the front of the vehicle; the other approached from the rear. Stacy didn't recognize either of them. She was boxed between the cars and the two men. There was no place to run. She shoved her bag at the man in front.

"Here, take my bag. There's only fifty-three dollars in it, but you're welcome to it." One of the men grabbed for the shoulder bag and slipped it over his own shoulder and took hold of Stacy's left arm. The other one grabbed her from behind, securing her right.

"It's not your money we'll be wanting, lass." Stacy's heart pounded in her head. She gasped for breath in short snatches attempting to break free of their grip. Between the two large men, she was easily shoved and pushed into the back seat of the sedan. She fell backward onto the seat, the doors slammed and the car roared off.

One of the men clicked cuffs over her wrists quickly and smoothly, being careful to not pinch her. The other hastily placed a blindfold over her eyes. Everything was happening so fast, she couldn't think straight. She tried to scream but shock wouldn't let any sound escape from her throat.

What did they want from her? What were they going to do with her? Did this have anything to do with the drug bust? Were these Gonzalo Quesada's thugs? Panic and fear consumed her. Her heart raced with dread. The men spoke not a word.

At last, the car stopped. A hand was placed on her head as she was guided out of the car. She could feel she was being steered upward on a ramp of some sort. It sounded hollow under her pumps. Water splashed in a steady rhythmic pattern. She was sure the sound was waves colliding with dock pilings. The smell of oil mixed with salt water invaded her nostrils. She knew the smell of a dock area. A loud ship's whistle startled her.

"Take her to the cabin before you take off the blindfold, Desfarges." Stacy recognized the voice at once. It was Ryan and this was no dream. What was going on? The rough hands guided her down the stairs and along a narrow passageway and into a cabin.

"Good work, guys. Take the blindfold off her." Stacy blinked to get her bearings. She couldn't believe her eyes. The cabin was overflowing with flowers. She sucked in her breath. The aroma of the mixture of flowers was intoxicating. The suite was beautifully done in tones of blue with peach draperies. Shiny chrome glass doors gave access to a private verandah. The three men and Ryan stood grinning down at her.

"What the hell is going on, Ryan Townsend?" she yelled at him. "You think you can just kidnap someone anytime you have a notion to do so. You're court bound, Mister."

One of the men, stuffing back a laugh, said, "I think we'll be going. Angry women always make me nervous."

"Yeah, thanks again guys. I couldn't have pulled this off without you." The men turned to leave the cabin. "Hope we weren't too rough, Miss," the sandy haired one said.

"Wait a minute," Stacy ordered. "You've got my purse." She snatched the bag off the man's shoulder.

"Excuse me, Ma'am."

She turned back to Ryan to continue her assault.

Ryan moved to take her in his arms.

She shoved him back. "You keep your paws off me. You, you, pirate," she snapped.

He pinned her arms behind her back, drawing her so close she couldn't move. She drew back a foot and let him have a swift kick in the shin.

"Damn it, Stacy. Calm down. It was the only way I could get you to listen to me. You wouldn't answer my calls or even return them."

"Return your calls? After the way you left me standing alone on that dance floor?"

"I know. I apologize for my behavior. I'm sorry."

"You're not nearly as sorry as you're going to be when my attorney gets through with you."

"Stacy, I love you. I'm not going to lose you.

Whatever it takes. You were right. If you weren't happy, I wouldn't be for long."

Stacy stopped fighting and relaxed on hearing his words.

"It's taken me a lot of sleepless nights to come to terms with that fact." His dark brooding eyes burned their way into Stacy's heart.

Stacy could feel sympathy moving in and despised herself for the weakness. She gritted her teeth and glared at him with contempt.

Ryan loosened his grip and continued. "Mitch put a Dutch uncle talk on me that made me realize I was being a male chauvinist. He didn't use those exact words." The grin began to sprout. "He said I was being a jackass. And Annie had already put in her bit—as only she can do."

"What bit? What do you mean, Ryan?"

"Annie said the secret to a good marriage was *fairness.* Stacy, I wasn't being fair. I was being a man wanting to protect you—to put you in a safe place and have everyone recognize what a great guy I was for doing it. I know now that's not love, it's ownership."

Tears threatened to spill over her dark lashes and spoil her mascara. She raised her fingers to his lips to hush his words.

"No," he said removing her hand. "Let me finish. You're good at what you do. I was proud of the way you handled the drug bust, but I was afraid for you, too.

I wanted to make the decision that you wouldn't ever be placed in a dangerous situation again. Mitch made me see that I have no right to make that decision."

Stacy looked steadily into his eyes. "Ryan, I could get run over by the St. Charles Avenue streetcar, have a car wreck and yes, even get cancer like Alice. No one has any guarantees. No matter how much you want to protect me, you can't."

"I know. I went through hell trying to take away the cancer from Alice. I wanted things to be the way they were supposed to be. I couldn't protect her anymore than I can you. It's hard for a man to face and accept the fact that there are some things he can't control."

He folded Stacy into his arms and held her close, swaying her gently back and forth. "I guess a woman's determination to have a career is one of them," he said with a resigned quiet laugh. "I'll learn to make compromises, Stacy."

"That's easier said than done, Ryan. A doting aunt and uncle who let you have your way most of the time raised you. Frankly, Mr. Townsend, you're a spoiled brat. You've never had to compromise a day in your life. I'm not sure you know what the word means."

"It's kinda like plea bargaining, isn't it?" He chuckled out loud, picked her up and nuzzled his face into her neck, placing kisses along the cord of her throat to her ear.

Stacy squirmed for freedom and snapped, "Ryan, this isn't funny. The happiness for both of us rests on this conversation."

Ryan set her on her feet but didn't relinquish his hold. He looked down into her eyes. They were shiny with moisture. "Stacy, I understand completely what you are saying. I know there'll be times when I want you with me and you'll have to cover some story. And there's going to be times when I have to be somewhere and you can't be there. What I'm trying to say is that I understand it's a two way street. As Annie put it—fairness."

Stacy smiled. A tear rolled off her cheek. She made an attempt to brush it away.

"No, from now on, I intend to kiss away those tears." Ryan bent and tenderly placed a kiss on her cheek and his lips traveled to hers and lingered passionately.

Stacy felt herself go weak in the urging power of his arms. "Ryan, Ryan . . ." His lips somthered her words. Hunger held back so long blazed.

A fist thundered against the cabin door quashing the moment. "Damn bad timing," Ryan hissed under his breath. He released her and opened the door. There stood Mitch with Danielle. Mitch held up two bottles of Dom Perignon and Danielle had a small Hartman suitcase.

"This is the Lafitte cabin I believe," Mitch said.

"Yeah, I guess you could say that." Ryan laughed. "I kidnapped her pirate style with the help of three undercover agents out of the A.G.'s office."

"Did you know about this, Mitch McGalliard?" Stacy asked, placing her hands on her hips and assuming her defiant stance. "Some friend."

"Well, I knew he had booked the cruise to St. Barts. I didn't know how he was going to get you on the ship."

Danielle set the luggage down and gave Ryan a big kiss. "I think it's the most romantic thing I ever heard of," she said. "Mitch, open those bottles, this ship will be leaving port soon."

Dutifully obeying, Mitch grabbed the sparkling champagne and began working on a bottle.

"There's supposed to be a tray of hor d'oeuvres in the fridge," Ryan said, moving to the small bar. He pulled out a silver tray loaded with cheeses, smoked salmon, boiled shrimp and a small package of rounds of dark bread. "This may turn into a great party," he said.

Danielle turned to Stacy. "When Mitch called and told me you were going to be taking a cruise on short notice. I thought you might need a few things. He sent me shopping. I hope everything fits. I guessed about a size four."

Stacy put her arms around Danielle. "Oh, Danielle, thank you. That's the right size." Stacy placed her hand across her forehead. "I haven't even considered clothes. I don't even have a toothbrush. As a matter of fact, I haven't said I'm going." Still overwhelmed, she said, "Everything has been a big blur since I walked out of the office."

Mitch handed a glass of champagne to Danielle and filled three more. "Oh, you're going all right. You've been so uptight this week, the office staff can't stand you anymore." Mitch said. "You need some time off to relax a while. He chuckled. "Now, whether you become Mrs. Ryan Townsend, I'll leave up to you two."

"Thank you very much for that, Boss." she said. "I guess my nerves have been a little exposed lately. I'm sorry if I've been a problem child, Mitch."

Danielle, with her female sense of wisdom, decided the subject should be dropped. "If I've overlooked something, there's a beautiful little boutique on board. Also, some great shops in the ports where you'll be stopping."

Mitch handed around champagne and raised his glass. "Here's to two people who deserve each other. Whether that's good or bad remains to be seen." The group laughed.

"Thanks a lot." Ryan raised his glass again and said quietly, "Here's to *fairness*." He stared directly into Stacy's eyes. Each smiled at the words and wisdom of the old black woman. Both knew she had given them the true secret to enduring happiness.

Stacy's eyes dampened and she gazed steadily at the floor to avoid the others eyes.

Mitch winked at Danielle and moved over to put his arm around her. "I think we missed something, Danielle." Danielle's eyes sparkled. She hadn't missed a thing.

"Is everything set for St. Barts?" Mitch asked.

"I'm not sure yet, I haven't had a chance to ask her. We still have some things to discuss," Ryan said.

Mitch said. "I'm going to go ahead and book our flight for St. Barts. If things don't work out, give me a call. I've got a hunch everything's going to be fine." He laid his hand on Ryan's shoulder. The ship's loud blast of steam signaled guests that the ship would be leaving the harbor shortly.

"We better be going." Mitch placed a kiss on Stacy's forehead, "Stacy, give him a chance. He really loves you."

Danielle hugged both Ryan and Stacy. "We'll see you in St. Barts," she said. "Have a wonderful cruise."

Ryan and Stacy walked them to the gangplank and waved as the ship pulled away from the dock of the Julia Street Terminal. The moon flickered over the waves making the light dance. Light also danced in Stacy's heart.

Ryan looked down at her, squeezed her hand. "Let's go finish that champagne."

"All right. Then you need to attend to some arrangements."

"Wedding arrangements?"

"No, not wedding arrangements. Don't play with me, Ryan Townsend."

"Whatever do you mean?" Ryan asked, opening his eyes wide trying to look innocent. He crossed the cabin to turn on the stereo attempting to focus the subject elsewhere. *Come Saturday Morning* drifted through the cabin.

"Don't play stupid with me. You know exactly I mean. You need to arrange for sleeping quarters for yourself. There's only one bed in this cabin and it's taken."

"Well, I thought you'd be a prude about it. So I've already arranged for the cabin across the hall. Now you can relax and enjoy the cruise."

"My nerves are raw. I could use the rest," she said.

"Here, this will make you sleep like a baby." He handed her a fresh glass of champagne and began to make finger sandwiches out of the salmon, cream cheese and rounds of bread.

"Hummm. This is wonderful, Ryan. I guess getting kidnapped gave me appetite. I didn't realize I was so hungry."

"Sorry, there's no potato salad. I told them to hold that," he laughed recalling the incident on the *Jury Room*. Stacy screwed up her face and stuck out her tongue at him.

They finished off the tray and the champagne.

"Stacy, I tried to give you this once before," he said pulling the diamond ring from his coat pocket. "I hope you accept it this time. Stacy, I love you more than I ever thought it was possible to love anyone. Please be my wife."

"Yes, Ryan, Yes . . . Yes," she breathed.

Ryan slipped Uncle Josh's "bauble" onto her finger, surrounded her with his arms pulling her close, and kissed her. His tongue explored the sweet mouth he had waited so long for. Slowly, he relished every crevice. Releasing her abruptly, he stepped back as if to place some distance between them before it was too late.

"Stacy, you need to get some sleep and so do I. You can't imagine how much work it is to pull off a kidnapping. I wish Uncle Josh could know that you said yes. He'd be dancing his little jig."

Stacy smiled. "I think he would too."

Ryan kissed her softly and tenderly once more and let her go.

"Listen, I'll knock on your door at eight. We'll go down and get some breakfast and take a walk around the deck. We have an appointment with the ship's doctor at nine for blood tests."

"Well, you were mighty sure of yourself," she said.

"I wasn't, but old Lafitte was." He winked, bent

over, gave her a quick peck on the nose and closed the door.

Stacy unsnapped the luggage case Danielle had brought. There were three short sets coordinated with a couple of pairs of slacks and a cardigan sweater. She hung up each piece after examining it and mentally putting the ensemble together. There was also a bathing suit with cover, sandals, and a pair of sneakers. Stacy sighed as she removed two dresses for evening with a pair of white strapped high-heeled sandals. One was white chiffon and the other a pale yellow silk, both Valentino. Danielle knew her clothes and didn't seem to worry about the price on the tag. Stacy found a little evening bag. Clicking it open, she discovered costume jewelry for the dresses.

A beautiful peach peignoir set lay in the bottom of the case. Stacy held it up to her, peered into the mirror, then swung around to see it float. It looked like peach ice cream. The most beautiful French lace lingerie Stacy had ever seen was in a plastic zippered bag. This must have cost a fortune. She continued to dig for the items that she was sure Danielle would have included. She found them in a side pocket—a toothbrush, paste, and a few items of makeup.

She'd never be able to repay Danielle for her thoughtfulness or Mitch, for that matter. Bosses like him don't come along often. She brushed her teeth and took a long hot shower but couldn't make herself put on the beautiful gown. She decided instead to sleep in her teddy. She'd go to the ship's boutique tomorrow and buy a big soft tee shirt, but for tonight the teddy would have to do.

If Ryan was going to knock on the door at eight she better set the alarm for seven. The clock was new and the buttons stiff. She broke a nail trying to get it set but in the end it complied. Falling into bed, she groaned, pulled the cover up under her chin. Her muscles were sore from the scuffle with the agents. She smiled thinking of the trouble Ryan had gone to. She stretched slowly like a cat then lay in the dark enjoying the rocking motion of the ship and the heady feel of the champagne. This had been the best day of her life—so far. She wrapped her arms around her body and gave herself a hug. She could wish for nothing more and drifted into a deep well-deserved sleep.

The sun peeped through the porthole above the bed. Stacy groaned, and turned over to checked clock. She stumbled into the shower. Warm water peppered down clearing the muddle from her brain. She chose the pair of navy slacks and white cotton knit sweater. In the pocket of the slacks, she found a gold nautical bracelet and earring set. That Danielle thought of everything.

Once dressed, she picked up a *Town and Country* magazine and flipped through the pages while she waited on Ryan. At eight sharp, a gentle rap sounded on the door. She rushed to open it.

Ryan stood there, grinning from ear to ear. "Hey, Danielle, did okay with those slacks. You look great."

"Thanks. You can't believe the beautiful things she put in that case. She and Mitch were beyond thoughtful. They'll never know how much I appreciate it."

"Me too," he said, and took a step back to get a better view of her derriere.

She laughed but avoided looking him in the face.

"Sleep good?" he asked.

"The waves rocked me to sleep. I must have slept hard. I feel more rested than I have in months."

"I'm starved. I hope they have eggs Benedict, waffles with maple syrup, ham biscuits with red eye gravy and blueberry muffins," he said.

"Good Lord," Stacy cringed, calculating the fat calories. "I hope you don't expect that every morning. I'm afraid you'll be disappointed."

"No, I'm just celebrating."

"Look," Stacy said, pointing to a strip of land on the starboard side of the ship. "What island is that?" It was lush with vegetation. Mountains rose in the background and water cascaded down. The light of the sun caught the falls, causing them to sparkle like a string of diamonds flowing to the sandy beaches.

"That's Jamaica. The ship docks in Montego Bay this morning. We can do some sightseeing and shopping if you like."

"Oh, yes, I'd love to."

"We'll be here all day, then the ship sails at ten tonight. We have to be back aboard by then."

Stacy ordered a bowl of cereal, whole-wheat toast, grapefruit juice and coffee. Ryan ordered every item he previously named but had to settle for cream gravy. Thoroughly enjoying himself, he devoured all of it.

"I'm ready for anything now," he said patting his stomach. "Except I'm not looking forward to getting poked with that needle." He squinted eyes as if in pain. "I suppose you're worth it. I wouldn't do it for just any girl you understand." His dark eyes crinkled with his grin. He reached over and squeezed her hand.

By nine thirty, both had given the blood samples.

"I need to drop by my cabin to get my sunglasses and cardigan before we go ashore," Stacy said.

"Okay, I'll grab another cup of coffee and meet you on deck."

When Stacy reached topside, Ryan was enjoying his coffee while talking to an older couple. He excused himself as soon as he saw her.

"Want another cup before we disembark?"

"No, I'm fine," she said. "I'm anxious to see the island."

"Did you see the couple I was talking to? They're celebrating their fiftieth wedding anniversary and having a ball."

The word "fiftieth" sawed on her brain. It sounded like a life sentence. Did anyone stay married for fifty years? Could she and Ryan make it? Uncertainty consumed her. Panic caused her heart skip a beat.

"Tell you what. We'll do this same cruise on our fiftieth anniversary." He hugged her close to him.

She smiled quietly at him, but said nothing.

Once they reached the street, Ryan unfolded a map. "Okay, Sam Sharpe Square is in that direction a couple of blocks."

"Ryan, I overheard some of the women on the ship talking about the duty free shops. I'd like to get Danielle a nice bottle of perfume."

"Good thinking. I'll take Mitch a couple bottles of Jamaican rum."

The shops bustled with tourists hastily gathering last minute items to take home. Windows glittered with crystal, china, porcelains and exotic perfumes. Stacy was trying to absorb the atmosphere all at once. They entered the Swiss Store. The mingling scents of the spicy perfumes heightened her senses.

It took Ryan about five minutes to make his purchase of the rum.

Stacy had to sample every perfume bottle on the counter. "Do you like this?" she asked holding up her wrist to let Ryan take a whiff of the perfume.

"Nice. What is it?"

"Bvlgari. I'll take the medium size," she told the

clerk. "And I want the Paris for myself. The small one, please."

"Hey, I didn't get to smell that one."

"Later," she said grinning up at him.

"Stacy, we really should pick out china and crystal patterns. We could save a bundle by purchasing it down here."

"There's no need for that, Ryan. The morning I made breakfast for you and Uncle Josh, I had to poke around to find dishes. There's beautiful china and crystal there."

"Yes, there is. Aunt Sue, Mother, and Grandmother had some magnificent things. I just thought you might want your own."

"I'd much rather use theirs if it's all right with you."

He placed his arm around her waist pulling her close to his side and planted a small kiss on her cheek. "I know they'd want you to."

"Ryan, could we go to Rose Hall? It's about eight miles just east of here."

"Sure, what is it?"

"It's a plantation with a wild history. I might be able to use it for a travel article."

"Don't you ever relax and enjoy what you see just for yourself? You seem to have to squeeze a reason out of everything you do."

"I can do both. That's what makes this profession

so great."

They rented a car and pulled out of the parking lot onto the street. Stacy's bloodcurdling scream ripped through the tranquillity of the morning. "What's wrong?" Ryan yelled. He jerked his head around to see what was going to hit them. Stacy had covered her face with her hands and braced her feet on the dashboard.

"Get over. You're on the wrong side of the road," she said.

Ryan took a deep breath to let his stomach return to its rightful position. Calmly, he said, "Stacy, in Jamaica people drive on the left."

A meek "Oh," followed. As if nothing had occurred, Stacy quickly became absorbed in the sur- roundings. The road was lined with vividly colorful hibiscus and bougainvillea. High-rise hotels and villas dominated the beach side of the road—luxurious, expensive, and touristy.

"Tell me about this Rose Hall," Ryan said.

"It was built in the 1770's. The second Mrs. Palmer, mistress of Rose Hall, murdered three or four husbands and had who knows how many lovers. She dressed in men's black clothes and rode horseback through the plantation at night. The legend says she still does. She participated in voodoo and even made lovers of her virile slaves. Some say it was one of them that murdered her."

Ryan chuckled. "Oh, is that all?" They pulled onto

the grounds.

"Ryan, this is a beautiful place." Peacocks strutted over manicured grounds. The gardens were ablaze with brilliant flowers. Stacy took notes as they toured the home. She paid particular attention to the docent's stories regarding the "White Witch" of Rose Hall. This was the name the slaves had given to Mrs. Palmer.

Ryan noticed four men walking up the driveway of the mansion. They didn't fit the image of tourists. They certainly didn't belong with the jeans and Nike crowd that usually sought out these tourists' stops. Their expensive designer sports clothes and Italian shoes would have more appropriate at a country club in Palm Beach. They looked as if they could have been tackles for a pro football team. Two had dark hair and eyes with olive complexions. One had brownish sandy colored hair with a lighter complexion and the last, flaming red hair. Ryan couldn't tell whether his eyes were blue or green but his complexion was florid. All were clean cut and well groomed. They appeared interested in the docent's explanations as well as the construction and design of the home, but they looked odd as a group.

The recent events caused Ryan to be aware of his surroundings at all times. Anything that seemed suspicious made his heart beat a little faster. He casually ran his hand across his jacket. The revolver resting under his arm comforted him. He didn't want to alarm Stacy. Besides, nothing would happen in this crowd. His imagination was probably working overtime. He took a deep breath and relaxed. He wasn't going to let his apprehension ruin the day.

Ryan smiled at her child-like inquisitiveness as she browsed through the gift shop. It was a joy to watch her enthusiasm. She approached life as a never-ending adventure. Marriage would not be dull with this girl.

Stacy purchased a bottle of perfume called "White Witch." She sniffed at it and held it up to Ryan to smell. The aroma was pungently floral but nice for summer nights she thought.

Returning to the parking lot, Stacy spied some wild orchids and wanted a closer look. She stopped to examine some of the blooms and asked the gardener the names of those she didn't recognize. The stooped shouldered little man was delighted she had taken the time to appreciate his work and both were enjoying talking about the plants.

Suddenly, a dark blue Buick slammed on its brakes and skidded to a stop. Three men jumped from the car and raced toward them. It was the same group that Ryan had noticed earlier. Two of the burly men wrestled Ryan to the ground. The other grabbed Stacy from behind, pinning her arm behind her back.

"Leave her alone. You hurt her, and I'll. . . ." A

sharp fire burned in Ryan's arm.

Stacy was forced into the back seat of the car. She turned to see Ryan slumped over the shoulder of one of the men and being carried to the car.

"What have you done to him?" she screamed and sunk her teeth into the hand that held her.

"Here, tie this bandanna over her mouth. Maybe it will keep you from being chewed up and we won't have to listen to her," the redheaded ruffian said.

They drove south, back through the market area of Montego Bay, out Howard Cooke Blvd. and Southern Cross Blvd, arriving at a marina on the peninsula. The car pulled to a gate with a guard holding a rifle and he motioned them through. They drove onto the dock area. Large fishing boats and yachts glistened in the afternoon sun. The car stopped in front of a sleek, streamlined craft, the engine already running. Stacy thought it looked like a fast boat. The plaque on the side read Ferretti 55. Ryan was hoisted on the redheaded man's shoulders and carried below. She followed, pushed along by her arm twisted behind her back.

Ryan was dumped on a bunk on one side of cabin. The sandy-haired man tied his hands and feet. Stacy was pushed down on the other bunk. The same thug tied her hands and feet as one of the other men held her. She struggled, but knew it was useless.

"Soon as we get you tied, Darling, you can have a

nice long nap."

She felt something jab her arm. Then blackness.

Ryan stirred as he regained consciousness. A rusty wrought iron bed squeaked loudly as he stirred. He was no longer on the boat. Boards covered the windows of some sort of shack. The sun slicing through cracks between the boards felt like an ax embedded in his brain. Music mingled in the next room with a mixture of Spanish and English.

He remembered hangovers before but nothing like this. The furniture in the room seemed to spin or was it him spinning? He wasn't sure. He felt nauseated from the smell of dirty musty mildewed sheets.

Turning his head, he discovered a mop of dark hair in his face. He groaned out Stacy's name. The grogginess began to clear. His eyes focused better. He watched Stacy's breathing to make sure she was still alive. *Just asleep.* He expelled a long breath that he hadn't been aware of holding. Relief swept across his face. They'd probably used the same stuff on her that they pumped into him. He tried to sit up, only to discover his hands and feet were bound. He strained against the ropes that entangled his hands. They were tied tightly cutting off the blood flow and causing a tingling sensation to creep through his fingers. He attempted again to right himself and this time was successful.

He pulled himself to a standing position, hopped over to a window to peep through the cracks. He could see blue water and a sandy beach. The cabin itself seemed to be located in the middle of a marshy area. A channel had been dredged through the marsh to let the boats have entry. A pier jutted out into water. A large yacht was moored to it. It looked as if at least one of the men was working around the boat. Water lapped against pilings underneath the floor. Ryan couldn't be sure the rhythmic throbbing sound wasn't just his brain knocking against his skull. Stacy groaned and stirred, then fell back asleep. Just as well, he thought.

In the distance, Ryan thought he heard the faint hum of a motor. It grew louder and louder. The cabin cruiser reduced its speed and the hum slowed as it reached the dock. Two of the attackers jogged down the pier to help moor the boat. This craft was much bigger than the first. Ryan calculated over eighty feet. Two men stepped onto the dock and turned to help an obese man with a cane onto the pier.

"Hey, Boss, you made pretty good time."

"Si, the Christensen not so fast as others but I must have my comfort. You have any trouble with our guests?" Quesada asked.

"No, they weren't expecting anything. We would have had a good fight on our hands without the drug. The woman's a real scrapper, bit Miguel's hand to the bone." Rusty laughed. "But they went right out when that needle hit them." The group made their way slowly up to the cabin as Quesada lumbered along. The cane made a hollow sound on the pier with each laborious step.

Chapter Eleven

*M*itch sat at his desk going over the day's schedule. The door opened and he looked up to see the copy boy standing in the doorway.

"Mr. McGalliard, this letter was hand delivered for you. They said it was urgent and that you should get it right away." Ted laid the envelope on Mitch's desk.

Mitch sliced open the envelope and removed its contents. His brows knitted together. He couldn't believe his eyes. He read the message a second time and picked up the phone.

"Chief Arcenaux, please, Mitch McGalliard calling. This is urgent. Don't put me on hold," he said sternly.

"Hey, Mitch what's up?"

"Chief, we've got problems. Ryan Townsend and Stacy Stimmons have been kidnapped. I think by Gonzalo Quesada, boss of the drug cartel out of Columbia.

"How do you know it's Quesada?"

"Because the bastard signed the note G.Q. He wants us to know. His way of thumbing his nose at us."

"You're probably right. If the word gets out that he will get even, he won't have to worry about anyone else giving him trouble. What does he want?"

"He wants seven and a half million for their return. The letter says that was the street value of the coke they lost in the bust."

"Seven and a half million? Whew, that's a lot of money."

"Mitch, you know they have no intention of returning Ryan or Miss Stimmons."

"Yeah, I know." He hesitated and added, "I think they want me, too. I'm supposed to fly to Jamaica with the money. There will be a contact at Sangster International to meet me."

"What makes you think they want you?

"Reference is made to my rudeness concerning some political toes I stepped on with articles printed in the *Picayune.*"

"You think the boys on this end are mixed up in this?"

"Don't you?" Mitch asked with a snort.

"Sounds like it could be some of Terrance Moody's shenanigans," Arcenaux said. "What are you going to do?"

"Hell. The only thing I can do. Get the money together and get my butt to Montego Bay," Mitch replied.

"Okay, I'll put a plan in motion. You're not as alone in this as you're going to feel for a while, Mitch."

"Don't let your men get too close, Arcenaux. There's no way to surprise them this time. These guys are real professionals. If they even think your men are close, Ryan and Stacy are dead."

"We'll be careful. You do the same, Mitch. We can't afford to loose you. You're a real hell raiser for a newspaper editor. It would be dull around here." The phone clicked.

Mitch grinned. He knew that was as close as he would ever come to getting a compliment out of Arcenaux. He raised the phone again to dial. This time—to Danielle.

"Mrs. Parker's residence."

"Percy, this is Mitch McGalliard. May I speak to Danielle?"

"Yes, sir. She just came down to breakfast. I'll tell her you're calling."

Mitch waited.

"Hello, Mi. . . ."

"Danielle, I don't have long. I'm not going to be able to make dinner tonight."

The feverish pace of his words told her something was wrong.

"What's wrong, Mitch?"

"Ryan and Stacy have been kidnapped."

"Oh, Mitch, don't do this to me. Enough is enough," she said disbelievingly.

"I'm not kidding, Danielle."

"Who—where?" she asked running her two questions together.

"We think it's Quesada's boys out of Columbia. The ship was scheduled to dock in Jamaica. That's where they want the money delivered, so I guess they must have gotten them when they disembarked."

"Quesada? I've met him. He attended meetings here at the house. Mean looking man. Dark, stubby, and overweight with a bad complexion. He makes you feel dirty just looking at you. What does he want?"

"Seven and a half million dollars."

"Seven and a half mill. . . ? Where are you going to get that much on such short notice?"

"That's the least of the worry. The paper has provisions and contacts for such emergencies. What bothers me is that the letter said they'd be just as pleased if I refuse to come. They'd just as soon kill Ryan and have him out of the way for future business dealings in New Orleans. Somebody out there knows he's got a good chance of following Anderson into the attorney general's office and they don't want that."

"But why would they want Stacy?"

"I'm afraid Stacy was just in the wrong place at the wrong time. If they kill him, they certainly can't let her go." He clenched his fist and released it. "Danielle, I don't know when I'll be back. I just wanted to call and tell you I love you."

Her voice strained. "Why do you have to go?" She knew the answer before she asked. Ryan would do the same for Mitch.

Mitch laughed. "They don't like my writing. The letter said if I didn't come, the deal was off. You know I have to go."

Her response was quiet and calm. "I know. It's just—I love you so much and we've waited so long. It doesn't seem fair. Please be careful, my love."

"You can count on it. We've got a lot of happiness to catch up on. I'm not going to let anything spoil it now, Danny. See you later." The phone went dead.

The slapping sound of cards and voices ceased in the adjoining room. The card game must be over Ryan thought. The door before him opened slowly and the three hoodlums Ryan had watched through the crack of the window entered. A nasty grin crossed the face of the younger one as he peered at Stacy's unconscious body. Ryan pulled himself to his feet and positioned his body between the intruders and Stacy. He stared unblinkingly at the man, all blubber-guts and ass, squeezing himself through the small portal.

"Señor Townsend, I have heard much of you. You make trouble for my business."

"Maybe you should consider changing businesses," Ryan answered. Two of the burly men made a move forward. Rusty, the red haired thug, knocked Ryan to the floor and said, "You keep your smart mouth shut, Townsend." The other kicked Ryan in the stomach with enough force to cause him double up in a heap.

A pair of alligator shoes stood eye level with Ryan.

"Please, please, Señor Townsend, there is no need for this unpleasantness. We are both gentlemen." Quesada shrugged his shoulders. "We each have our jobs to do."

Ryan's eyes traveled up the blue-gray suit until they reached the pocked scared face, punctuated by a sneering smile. His bloated skin was shinny with the combination of humidity and heat. It made him look as if he were melting. In spite of the expensive clothes, the greasy appearance and slicked down hair made him appear dirty. He reeked of garlic. The smell sent waves of nausea through Ryan's battered stomach. Ryan had seen the man before. It had been at a meeting of Mafia members at Roland Parker's home. The man smelled the same way then.

"Where are your manners, muchachos? Help

Señor Townsend into the chair."

Grabbing him by the arms still tied behind his back, the two ruffians jerked Ryan off the floor, and heaved him into the chair. Blood ran in a trickle from the corner of his mouth. Dazed, he ran his tongue over the split lip.

"You know, Roland Parker was a good amigo of mine, Señor," Quesada said. "We trusted each other. If money was a little late getting out of New York, I let Roland have the product on his word. He always kept it—until the last time."

"Yeah, a real honorable businessman. That was Roland all right." The movement of Ryan's lips caused the blood to run in a steady flow.

"The business we had going in New Orleans could have been a profitable venture for us for a long time. You could have profited also, Mr. Townsend. Roland had big plans for your political career."

Stacy stirred, groaned and groggily opened her eyes. She tried to focus on the shadowy figures. She heard their muffled voices, but couldn't understand the conversation. She tried to sit up and discovered her hands and feet were bound.

"Ryan, Ryan," she moaned. One of the thugs moved to her and carefully brushed his hand across her face pushing the hair from of her eyes.

"She's very pretty, Boss. Could be nice company for us on the trip back to Santa Marta."

227

"Get your filthy hands off her," Ryan spat.

The force of the goon's backhand lifted him from the chair. Blood spurted again. Ryan's head slumped to his chest.

Stacy's thoughts were slowly clearing. Now she remembered the abduction. Her arms and shoulders were sore from the rough handling she'd received. She attempted to stretch away the soreness. "What are you going to do with us?" she asked weakly.

The fat man answered. "Ahh, Miss Stimmons. How do you feel?"

"How do you think I feel?" she hissed at him.

"It's unfortunate that you were with Mr. Townsend. Oh, we know you were included on the drug bust that cost Mr. Parker his life and your article in the paper hurt our feelings. We were not happy about that—but you were only doing your job. We understand these things." The man grinned, showing teeth badly in need of a dentist.

Stacy's skin crawled as the huge man's eyes traveled over her body.

Ryan regained consciousness and shook his head to clear his senses. "What do you think you're going to gain from this?" he asked.

"Seven and a half million dollars, Señor, your and Miss Stimmons hides, plus the corpse of Mitch McGalliard," came the response from Quesada.

"What are you talking about?" Stacy asked.

228

"The original plan was to put only you on ice, Señor Townsend. Miss Stimmons got in the way, so we have no choice but to include her. Then Terrance came up with a better plan. Mr. McGalliard's paper printed articles that didn't help his political aspirations. This gets rid of all the problems once and for good. Much neater, you see."

It was now apparent who was responsible for the kidnapping. It didn't surprise Ryan. Even in Angola, it looked as if Moody was still operating.

"A letter was delivered to the *Picayune* this morning with instructions for your 'safe' return. Señor McGalliard is bringing us the money in exchange for you. Do you think you are worth seven and a half million dollars?" Quesada asked.

"You're out of your mind, Quesada," Ryan said. "Don't you think the authorities know you'll kill us anyway? Mitch won't fall into a trap like that. He's too smart for that one."

"You're right, of course. But Señor McGalliard is consumed with—how you say? Ahh, yes—morals. He's too loyal a friend to let you die. You're a lucky man, Señor." Quesada waggled his finger in the air. "Not many men would lay their life on the line for an amigo. Smart or no, he's coming."

Stacy felt a tear threatening to overflow her lashes and roll down her cheek. Of course, he would come. He loved Ryan like a brother. She brushed her cheek against her shoulder to eliminate the droplet. The worse thing she could do was show weakness now.

Quesada pushed back his monogrammed sleeve to check his Rolex. "Señor McGalliard should be landing in a couple of hours. Cordero, it will take you about that to get back to Montego Bay. Dock at the same place and pick him up at Sangster International. He's coming in on American flight 898."

"How will I know him, Boss?" Cordero asked.

Quesada showed the decayed toothy grin and said, "Just write 'McGalliard' on a piece of cardboard. Hold it up as the passengers leave the gate. He'll find you— pronto."

"Si. Good thinking, Boss."

"Is why I am Boss," Quesada muttered matter-of-factly. "Cordero, take Miguel and Naldo with you. And Cordero, there's no need for Señor McGalliard to be brought back to Pedro Cay. He will make a nice dinner for the fishes."

Cordero laughed under his breath. "I understand, Boss."

"When you have the money and the problem laid to rest, head for Santa Marta. We'll take these two with us."

"You have the same plan for us, don't you, Quesada?" Ryan said.

"Señor Townsend, you behave yourself and maybe we let Miss Stimmons go when we reach Santa Marta."

"Sure you will." Ryan's brain wrestled for a workable solution to destroy Quesada's plan.

Stacy knew that Quesada was lying. There was no way they could let her go after what she had witnessed. Besides, without Ryan, what was there to live for? She took in a deep breath and exhaled it with a sigh.

"Edwardo, you and Mateo get them on the boat," the big man ordered.

Edwardo, the taller of the two, knelt and untied Ryan's feet. He yanked Ryan out of the chair and shoved him towards the door.

Ryan looked around in time to catch Mateo, the youngest of the group, run his hand over Stacy's breast. He saw Stacy close her eyes and swallow hard. Ryan set his jaw in a hard line as rage raced through his veins. He had never felt the urge to kill before but there was no mistaking the exploding madness.

The dark young man whispered something in Stacy's ear and smiled lecherously at her.

Stacy drew back from the grinning vile creature as he pulled her from the bed and pushed her toward the door. Outside, they were shoved and prodded down the pier, onto the awaiting Christensen and below into a stateroom. A berth lay along the hull on each side of the cabin.

"Here, lady. You stay here." The hoodlum made a motion for her to lie down. Trembling, Stacy did as Mateo ordered.

Ryan had been placed on the other berth. He watched the grinning whelp. Mateo unzipped Stacy's slacks. Her body gave an involuntary shudder. He ran his hand under her lace panties all the while grinning at Ryan and watching for his reaction. Ryan's dark eyes turned to steel as violence burned in his brain.

"Mateo, get up here," Edwardo yelled. "Boss wants you." Mateo went topside.

"Stacy, are you all right?" Ryan asked.

She turned her face toward him not really wanting to meet his eyes and needing to be close to him at the same time. "I'm all right. Don't be a hero, Ryan. I don't want you hurt anymore." Tears cascaded down her cheek as she gazed at his battered face.

One of his eyes had already swollen shut. Blood continued to trickle from his cut lip. It had run down his neck and dried on the collar of his shirt. She wanted to touch him and tend his wounds. The ropes wouldn't let her move. The ropes cutting into her wrists had cut off the blood circulation. Her hands were numb. The only thing she could do was let the tears fall and she knew she must not. Stop it, she commanded herself.

Mateo descended the stairs and entered the state-room. He held two syringes.

"Boss say maybe better you sleep." He jabbed Ryan in the arm and turned to Stacy. She strained against the ropes but it was useless. The drug did its work immediately.

Mitch's plane touched down on schedule. Carrying only a large soft travel bag, he descended the stairs into the humid tropical climate. He could already feel his damp clothes cling to his body. Maybe, it was just nerves. A steel reggae band welcomed tourists to the island. Mitch looked around, trying to discover anyone who might be attempting to gain his attention. He had no idea what his connection looked like. He wandered with the crowd of tourists through the terminal. Momentarily, he spied a man holding up a board with "McGalliard" printed on it. He was sturdily built and wore white slacks, a golf shirt, and a mint green linen blazer. Mitch was all too aware of why the blazer bulged under his left arm. He took a deep breath and approached the man.

At Mitch's arrival, the man said, "Señor McGalliard?"

"Yeah."

"My name is Cordero. You will follow me, please. May I take your bag for you?"

"No, thanks. I can manage just fine." Mitch knew that with this many people around he was safe in refusing the hoodlum's request.

"How far do we have to go?"

"We must go to another island, Señor. Your friends are there."

"Are they all right?"

"But of course, Señor," Cordero said.

"I think I'd better go to the toilet before we leave the airport," Mitch said.

"It is this way, Señor." The men entered the lavatory.

"Wait, Señor." Cordero ran his hands over Mitch's body looking for a gun. Mitch hadn't bothered to carry a gun. Arcenaux had offered to get it cleared with airline security, but Mitch knew it would be of little use. He was certain he would be searched. He hoped they wouldn't find the wire and the minuscule homing device sewn into the lapel underlining of his jacket.

When Mitch emerged from the stall, he noticed a man standing before a basin busily washing his hands. Mitch stepped to the basin beside him to do the same. Cordero leaned against the wall near the door waiting for Mitch to finish. Mitch caught the man looking intently into his eyes through the mirror. Instantly, he knew what it meant. Arcenaux is here. Hope they don't screw this up he thought. He dried his hands and rejoined Cordero.

A dark blue Buick waited at the curb. Cordero opened the back door and gave Mitch a shove into the back seat. Naldo was waiting in the back with a pistol pointed at Mitch's stomach. Mitch was placed in the middle. Cordero slid in beside him. The driver dropped the car into gear and it sped off. It moved down Queens Drive towards town, out Howard Cooke Blvd onto Southern Cross passing the Bob Marley Performing Center. They hadn't bothered to blindfold him. Mitch wondered why, but not for more than second. It became obvious. He wouldn't be coming back. The car passed through a security gate and stopped on the large pier of a marina.

"This is where we get out, Señor," Cordero said. "We will take the boat to the island."

The craft stood waiting. "Looks like a fast boat. How long will it take us to get there?" Mitch asked, trying to get a timetable from Cordero. If the authorities knew the time it would take, it would give them a pretty good idea of where the boat was going.

"Not as fast as the cigarette boat, but doesn't call as much attention either. It will do thirty knots." Cordero didn't answer Mitch's question. He took Mitch by the arm and escorted him onto the boat. The other two followed. One kept nudging him in the back with something small and hard. It didn't take a genius to know it was a gun. It would be foolish to try anything. He did exactly as they directed. He was shown below to a stateroom.

"Now Señor McGalliard, I will take the bag," Cordero said jerking it out of Mitch's hand. Mitch turned the lapel containing the mike toward Cordero as he handed over the key to the bag.

"Which island are we going to?" Mitch tried again.

Cordero zipped the bag open. His eyes glazed over as he looked at the money and smiled.

"You know Jamaica well, Señor?" Cordero asked.

"I've been down here on vacation a few times. I like to come for the scuba diving and the fishing."

"Yes, many visitors come. We go to Pedro Cay. The fishing is good there."

Mitch hoped the authorities had heard that.

"Now Señor McGalliard, take off your jacket and make yourself comfortable. The heat can be exhausting. Relax and enjoy the ride. I will have Naldo bring you a cool drink."

Mitch didn't want to remove his jacket but he was afraid they might get suspicious if he didn't. He took off the jacket and laid it on the other berth with the lapel facing up to hide the wire and homing device. Maybe it would pick up something.

Naldo entered the stateroom and handed Mitch a cold can of Michelob. The beer was icy and Mitch welcomed it as it slid down his throat. Naldo returned topside. Mitch finished the beer and stretched out on the berth. He wished he could drop off to sleep but that wasn't likely.

They had been traveling about an hour when the motor of the boat died. Waves no longer slapped the hull. Mitch sat up as Cordero descended the steps into the stateroom.

"I am sorry to disturb you, Señor McGalliard."

Miguel and Naldo followed Cordero down and positioned themselves on either side of Mitch.

"I'm afraid it is time to feed the fish. They requested 'gringo' meat." The thugs laughed. Naldo and Miquel grabbed Mitch by the arms and shoved him back up the stairs and onto the deck. He struggled against them. Something crashed into his head. Then the clear blue water splashed. Mitch's mouth went salty and cool water cleared his head. He'd been thrown overboard. The motor of the boat turned over and caught. Propellers shot water out behind the boat and it lunged forward. Cordero yelled back, "Don't worry, Señor McGalliard. You won't be here long. The teeth of the sharks will be tickling your toes any minute now." Laughter erupted from the vessel. With mixed emotions Mitch let his loafers slide off his feet and sink to the bottom. It would be easier to stay afloat without them or the weight of his slacks. He unbuttoned the waist, unzipped and pulled them off. They floated on top for a while then slowly sank. He watched as the boat disappeared into the distance. Had Arcenaux been able to hear the bug? Were they following the boat? How long could he tread water?

It seemed as if hours passed. *Damn it. Where are those guys?* Mitch felt as if his arms would fall off. He almost wished his legs would. They were enormously heavy and ached unbearably. His scissors kick had slowed its pace so much it was nearly nonexistent. He tried to relax and float.

Danielle's gently smiling face flashed across his mind and he prayed, "Please God, not now. This isn't fair. We deserve our time together." He returned to treading water with renewed purpose, at the same time conserving as much of his strength as he could.

He wondered if Stacy and Ryan were still alive. He remembered the first day Stacy had stepped into his office looking like a runway model, only about seven inches too diminutive. Her dark eyes had snapped with enthusiasm. He had recognized her spunk and ambitious grit under the too perfect cover. When she kept turning up week after week, he was convinced that she was persistent enough to get any story he would send her to cover. She hadn't let him down. He needed some of her spunk now.

He thought he heard the sound of a motor somewhere, but he didn't see a boat in any direction. The noise grew louder and louder. The steadiness of the sound developed into a swoosh—swoosh—swoosh. It was coming from overhead. A helicopter hovered. By now, the sun had burned Mitch's face and eyes badly. His vision was blurry, but he could see two figures jump from the copter. He heard them hit the water causing a huge wave to roll over his head choking him.

Someone grabbed him under the arms. The other secured a canvas seat around him. Slowly the seat ascended with him and one of the men. When he was snatched into the helicopter, the first thing he saw was Arcenaux's grinning face.

"Hey Bro, enjoy your swim?" The nervous laugh that escaped from Arcenaux's mouth was one of relief.

"Man, am I glad to see you. Where have you been? I thought I'd had it." Mitch leaned out and heaved, expelling a cup of salt water. Arcenaux wiped Mitch's mouth with a towel.

"You said not to get too close. We were just following your instructions."

"Next time, ignore what I say, please." Mitch grinned. He was regaining some of his strength.

"Did you hear? They have Ryan and Stacy somewhere in the Pedro Cay area."

"Yeah, we heard. We have copters and boats from the Navel-Air Station at Guatammo Bay combing the area now. We've called for backup to keep following the boat that dumped you. I want to get you back to shore to a doctor."

"No, we don't have time. I'm all right. Let's keep following."

The pilot interrupted, "Chief, we don't have much fuel left. We'll have to return to Montego Bay."

"Damn," Mitch said.

"Don't worry, McGalliard. I promise you, we'll get these bastards. Is that jacket of yours still on board?"

"I guess so. It didn't go overboard with me," Mitch said.

"I imagine by now, one of those guys has it on," Arcenaux said. "He'll lead us straight to them. It's just a matter of time."

"Yeah, but that's the problem. How much time do we have, Chief?"

Chapter Twelve

The drug slowly wore off. Ryan awoke with the same groggy feelings that accompanied an all night drunk. He remembered the needle. Pain exploded behind his eyes. The swaying of the boat made him want to throw up.

"Stacy, are you awake?" He had trouble getting his tongue to work in co-operation with his lips. Twisting his hands, he tried to loosen the ropes. Soon he had worn all the skin off his wrists, leaving them raw and burning.

"Stacy." He waited a few seconds and called her name again. "Stacy."

Stacy groaned weakly and answered. "Ryan, I feel so lousy."

"Yeah, I know, but you've got to wake up. I think my ropes may be loosening a little. Do you think you can sit up and untie them with your teeth?"

"I'll try." Stacy attempted to lift her body to a sitting position on the berth. Her head weighed a ton. She sank back.

"Ryan, I'm so sleepy. Please let me sleep."

"No, Stacy. Damn it, wake up. How bad do you want to live, woman?"

He had never used this tone of voice with her. He sounded angry and pleading at the same time. Stacy lifted her head and tried once again. This time, she sat up but was shaky. She dropped her bound feet over the edge of the berth and they hit the floor with an uncontrolled thud. She cringed hoping the sound wasn't heard above and she dropped to her knees on the floor beside Ryan's bunk. He turned as far around as he could to enable her to get at the ropes. She clasped her incisors over the top rope and pulled. The hemp fiber scoured her lips raw, but she continued to bite at them and pull.

"Wait, I think I feel it giving," Ryan said.

She stopped. "Don't try to pull them apart yet. I can see the top rope is loosing a little. I think I can give you enough slack that you can get them apart in just a minute." She tasted blood but resumed gnawing at the ropes. "There, try it now."

Ryan pulled his hands apart and finished untangling the rope. He untied his feet, then her hands.

"Can you get your feet untied?" She nodded yes and went to work on the ropes.

Ryan looked around the cabin searching for something they could use as weapons. Anything. "Stacy, check those drawers at the back of the cabin and see what you can find. I'll try to get this hanging locker open." The locker had a padlock on it.

Stacy opened the drawers as quietly as she could. All she found was a windbreaker, socks, and some men's underwear. The next contained tee shirts. The last was stuffed with papers, maps, nuts and bolts, screws, and small used parts of metal. In the corner of the drawer her fingers felt a Phillips screwdriver and she freed it from a tangle of string.

"I need something to break open this lock," Ryan said. He remembered the Cross-pen he had in his jacket pocket. He inserted it into the staple portion on the hasp. That looked like the weakest point. The pen cracked and broke into two pieces. "Damn."

"Here try this," she said, shoving the screwdriver towards Ryan.

He took it and Stacy continued to rummage through the drawer. It reminded her of a small boy's pockets—a few marbles, a rusty washer, a dime, nickel, two pennies, and yesterday's chewed gum wrapped in tin foil for later. Then she winced and pulled her hand back. The tip of one finger was bloody. She popped it into her mouth to stifle the sting and then dug deeper. Her hand withdrew a hunting knife. "Look, what I found."

"Let me see."

She held it up to hand it to him.

"You keep the knife. I'll use the screwdriver. It won't cut but if I use enough force, it'll go deep."

"Ryan, I don't want to do this."

"Well, you think I do? Look Stacy, we don't have any choice. Once they throw us overboard, it's all over."

He continued to try to pry the lock off with the screwdriver. It wouldn't give. Sweat soaked the back of his shirt. Stacy wasn't sure if it was from exertion and humidity—or fear. She was sure hers was pure panic.

The hasp gave a painful scraping sound and then a pop as it pulled away from the locker. Ryan opened the door, took a quick peek and closed it. "That racket might bring somebody down here. Get back on your bunk."

Stacy jumped back into the bunk as Ryan righted the hasp in an attempt to make it look intact. Quickly he returned to his bunk and positioned his hands and feet to appear tied. They had no sooner made their retreat when Mateo scampered down stairs.

"What was that noise? What are you doing down here?" he asked while slowly glancing around the cabin. Once convinced everything was all right, he placed his attention on Stacy. He smirked and bent over her to touch her face.

Ryan sprang from the berth. He clasped his hand tightly over Mateo's mouth to stifle any sound and shoved the screwdriver deep through the mobster's ribs. Mateo groaned and slumped to the floor. He gave two deep gasps then lay still.

Stacy stammered, "Is—Is he dead?"

Ryan didn't answer. He leaped over the corpse and pulled open the hanging locker. There were a couple of scuba tanks with fins and goggles. A spear gun with spear lay in the back of the locker.

"Know how to use one of these things?" He pumped it once and shoved it at her.

"I never have."

"All you have to do is point that thing and pull the trigger right here." He placed her finger on the trigger. "Is it too heavy?"

"No, I can manage," she said.

"By my count, we have one piloting the boat. Quesada is probably in the other stateroom either sleeping or eating."

Stacy said, "That leaves the red headed one unaccounted for. He could be anywhere."

"Yeah, this is what we'll do," Ryan said. "Give me the knife. Our only hope is to get control of the boat before they know what's happening. Stand in the stairwell and cover me with the spear gun. If I make it to the wheel I'll turn the boat around slowly. If they're taking afternoon siestas, they may never know we've turned."

"What do you want me to do then?"

"If I get that far, come on up on the bridge. We play it by ear from there, Sweetheart. Here I go."

Ryan slid silently up the stairs and onto the deck. The second flight of stairs to the bridge lay in front of him. Edwardo stood with his back to Ryan, piloting the boat. With the wind and the sound of the engine, Edwardo didn't hear Ryan ascend the steps. Ryan grabbed him, placing his hand over his mouth just as he had Mateo. Edwardo struggled. A shot rang out.

"Oh God." Stacy scampered up the stairs as fast as she could to the bridge. Ryan lay in a heap. Blood gushed from his head. Edwardo was crumpled up on the floor also. His eyes were opened wide and glared into space. A gurgling noise escaped his limp body. Ryan had managed to cut the thug's throat before Edwardo pulled the gun and fired.

"Ryan, Ryan, please God no," she moaned. His body lay in a lifeless heap. She fell to the deck and held his head in her lap. Blood ran from the side of his head and laced its way through her fingers. Looking down into his pale face, she pushed his dark hair from his eyes. She rocked him back and forth in her arms holding him close and crying softly, "Ryan, Ryan."

She detected no sign of life.

Someone ran across the deck in rubber soled shoes. He stopped at the bottom of the stairs leading to the bridge. Stacy caught her breath. Slowly she drew herself to her feet trying to be as quite as possible. Then darted to the other side of the bridge, away from the wheel and the bodies.

If he was coming up, his eyes would be focused on the wheel. She stood as still as she could and glanced again at Ryan. There was nothing she could do for him. Then she caught a glimpse of Edwardo's gun under the edge his body. She couldn't get to it without being seen.

The gangster slowly ascended the stairs. Stacy could hear him coming step by step. She would only have one shot with the spear gun. If she could get a clear view of his upper body she would have a better chance than trying for his head. But would she have time? She needed surprise on her side. She prayed she had guessed right and he would be looking in the direction of the wheel when he came up the last step.

"Edwardo. Edwardo?" the man called. Stacy held her breath; afraid the sound of her breathing might be heard. She stood poised to let the spear fly. His flaming red hair protruded from the floor of the bridge as he continued to climb the stairs. Then Stacy saw his face.

His blue eyes were opened wide and bulged with fear. She saw him glance at the wheel, then at

Edwardo's body. She concentrated, waiting until he exposed enough of his upper body. It seemed to take an eternity. One more step. Holding the gun firmly against her shoulder, she squeezed the trigger and the lance took flight. It hit the man's chest with a thud and made a sucking sound. He screamed once and fell backwards onto the deck below.

Stacy sprang across the bridge and shoved Edwardo off the gun. She grabbed it and pointed it at the stairway. If they had counted correctly, only Quesada was left. She picked up the microphone on the radio and pushed the on button.

"May Day. May Day. Please, come in, please." All she heard was static. She repeated the message. Then the sound of the cane tapping its way across the deck caught her attention.

"We hear you. Come in. Come in," came the voice from the radio.

"Miss Stimmons?" Quesada called up the steps. "Please come down, Miss Stimmons. You can not escape. Where is Señor Townsend?"

Stacy's heart sank. Desperation set in. Her insides trembled uncontrollably. She closed her eyes tightly. A single tear rolled down her cheek. Ryan was dead, but Quesada didn't have to know that.

She stuffed back the sobs and remained silent. He must not know where she was. Bullets could easily penetrate the flooring of the bridge. She must think.

From the sound of his voice, she gambled that he stood at the bottom of the stairs. There was no way the big man could scale them alone.

"Miss Stimmons, you know I can not climb to the bridge, but I have plenty of bullets to shoot. Sooner or later, I will hit you."

She knew he was right. She had to make a decision and act fast. The deck exploded and chunks of wood sang covering her feet. Splinters gouged their way under her skin and she jumped back. He began shooting wildly up through the bridge. She heard his cane scrape the wall. He was trying to climb the stairs.

She dove towards the edge of the bridge, landed on her stomach and emptied the gun down the stairs. Silence. It was so still. All she heard was sound of the engine idling and gentle waves slapping at the boat. The wind blew a lock of hair into her mouth. She slapped at it to dislodge it.

Cautiously, she peered down the stairs onto the deck. Quesada lay doubled up in a huge ball covered with blood. A groan came from behind her. She jerked around with the gun pointed and ready even though it was empty. Ryan's body moved.

"Ryan," she rushed to him and bent down. "Ryan, I thought you were dead."

He moved his lips in a faint whisper.

"Don't talk. I'll get help." She said and took the microphone again. "May Day. May Day. Come in, please. I need help. May Day. May Day." Static came again.

"We hear you. We hear you. Where are you?"

"I don't know. My name is Stacy Stimmons from the *Picayune* in New Orleans. I have an injured man that needs medical attention immediately. We're on a large yacht headed for Santa Marta from the Jamaica area. That's all I know."

"Miss Stimmons, we've been looking for you. We can't be far from you."

"I don't know anything about driving this boat. Should I wait for your arrival?"

"We can get you help faster if you move the yacht toward Jamaica. You can do it. Just listen carefully. Take the helm."

Oh God, please give me strength she prayed silently. "I'll try. Yes, I have it."

"There's a lever you need to push a little bit forward. This will give you some speed. Turn the helm until your compass arrow is on North. Do that, then I'll give you the next step."

"Okay, here goes." Stacy's hand shook as it grasped the lever and pushed it forward. The engines roared louder and the boat moved forward. The compass told her she was headed almost due South. She turned the wheel slowly while watching the compass. "Okay, the compass is on the N."

"Great, now keep that compass needle right there.

Shove the throttle forward as far as it will go. Push the auto pilot button beside the wheel and bring that baby home."

"Wait. Wait. I can't dock this thing."

"You won't have to. We'll intercept you before long. When you see us, just pull back slowly on the throttle until we get close. Then turn off the key. Just like your car. We'll tie up to you."

"Okay, I can do that."

Ryan had pulled himself to a sitting position and held his head in his hands. Blood oozed, sticking to his fingers.

Stacy put the lock on the helm to keep the boat headed in the right direction. So much blood. She had to get it stopped. Hastily, she began to look around for a first aid kit. There had to be one. Yes, it hung on the wall. She opened it and removed gauze, scissors and antiseptic. She squirted the antiseptic onto the wound.

Ryan flinched. "That burns."

"Be still. I have to get this bandage tight to stop the bleeding." She wrapped Ryan's head. "How are you feeling?"

"Dizzy. My head hurts like hell."

"Don't talk anymore. Help's on the way. We're going to be fine." Stacy kissed him with passion as if trying to give him all her strength. He had to be all right.

In the distance, Stacy saw the white ship flying an American flag. "Thank God," she whispered. She let the boat run full throttle as close as she dared, then cut the engine as she had been instructed.

Several sailors boarded and began searching the boat. A medical team went to help Ryan immediately. They placed him in a basket and carried him aboard the U.S. vessel. A uniformed officer approached Stacy.

"I'm Captain Cooper with the U.S. Coast Guard. These men know what they're doing. Don't worry, Miss Stimmons, he's in good hands." He looked about at the bodies littering the deck of the yacht. "Lord, lady, what happened here?"

Stacy told him everything that had happened since the kidnapping began.

"Are you all right? Can you make it aboard?" he asked.

"Yes, I'm shaken pretty good, but I'll be fine."

"We have a chopper on the way to transport you and Mr. Townsend to Doctor's Hospital at Montego Bay. The boys will tend to the wound and make sure he's stabilized."

One of the medics placed a blanket around her shoulders, "Want an injection for your nerves?" he asked.

"No, I've had all the injections I want for a while, thank you very much but I would really appreciate a cup of hot coffee."

"Yes, ma'am. I'll get it right away."

"You sit right here and enjoy your coffee," Captain Cooper said.

Stacy said, "I'd like to check on Mr. Townsend, please."

"Willis, get a report on Mr. Townsend," the captain ordered to a sailor.

"Yes, sir." The young man disappeared.

The steaming hot liquid tasted delicious and comforting going down. She shivered and savored the taste. Realization that she and Ryan were safe began to sink in. Stacy offered a simple but sincere, "Thank you, God."

The young sailor returned and reported to his captain. "They have the bleeding under control and have dressed the wound. He's been given a sedative and is asleep."

"Thank you, Willis." Captain Cooper turned to Stacy.

"He'll be more comfortable for transporting if he's asleep."

The sound of the helicopter's blades swooshed overhead. The whirly-bird set down easily on the deck. They had Ryan prepared. He would be loaded as soon as it touched.

The door of the chopper opened, and out jumped Arcenaux.

Stacy blinked twice to make sure she was seeing

what she was seeing. She was overjoyed to see a familiar face. His presence had a way of conveying that everything was under control.

"Miss Stimmons, y'all okay?"

"I'm fine, but Ryan's hurt. How did you get here?"

"Oh, I had to come make sure Mitch handled things right. He gets himself in all kinds of trouble." The chief grinned.

In all the confusion, Stacy had forgotten Mitch.

"Is he okay? Did they hurt him?"

"He's fine. Just a little waterlogged." Arcenaux laughed.

"Where is he?" Stacy asked.

"He's waiting at the hospital for us."

"At the hospital? You're sure he's okay?"

"I'll tell you all about it once we get you and Townsend on the copter."

Stacy thanked the captain and the crew, boarded the helicopter and waved as it rose.

Mitch sat in a wheelchair with a young black Jamaican nurse standing behind him at the edge of the helicopter pad at Doctor's Hospital.

"I can wait by myself," he said to the nurse. "I hate to take up your time when someone else might really need you."

"You're an important patient, Mr. McGalliard and we always take the best care of our VIPs," she answered.

Mitch had been given the report that Stacy was just shaken, but Ryan had a head injury. They didn't know the extent of the injury. Mitch's brain spun in apprehension. Ryan could be a brain damaged or paralyzed. He might even die. He had to be okay. Mitch knew he had to think positively. Stacy would need his support through this.

His thoughts spun to Danielle. He'd call her as soon as he knew something. He smiled. He had something special he needed to ask her. But first, he must know Ryan's condition.

The chopper was coming in. Help flooded out the side door of the hospital instantly. They placed Ryan on a gurney and rolled him into an examining room. He was unconscious. Mitch thought Ryan looked awfully gray. Stacy climbed out of the machine accompanied by Arcenaux. She smiled weakly at him and bent down to throw her arms around him. "Mitch, how are you?"

"I'm fine. It's just hospital rules that I get a chauffeured ride in this thing. They want to keep me overnight for observation. How's Ryan?"

"He regained consciousness on the boat. He's lost a lot of blood. I really couldn't tell how deep the wound is. They wouldn't let me around him on the Coast Guard boat. That's all I know until they examine him."

Arcenaux said, "Come on. We'll go with him as far as they'll let us."

An imposing nurse with the voice of a top sergeant stopped them and they were shown to a waiting room.

"Stacy, can you give me a statement?" Arcenaux asked.

Stacy described the kidnapping in as much detail as she could. When she got to the part about the spear gun, Mitch interrupted her.

"Good God, Stacy, you killed a guy with a spear gun?"

"I had no choice, Mitch. That's not all. I killed Quesada too."

"Good for you," Arcenaux said. "That'll save the taxpayers a bundle."

The ever-present newsman in Mitch came alive. "Stacy, what a story. You know you've got another headliner."

"I don't ever want another, if I have to get it like that, Mitch."

"Can't say I blame her there," Arcenaux said.

"Did they get the guys that had you?" she asked Mitch.

Arcenaux answered, "Yeah, that was easy. They gave up without a fight when those boats and choppers surrounded them."

Several hours went by. Stacy lost count of how

many cups of coffee she had. Arcenaux and Mitch tried to keep her spirits up with light conversation. She knew they were as worried as she was.

Finally, a doctor stepped out of the examining room. They stood as he approached. There was a slight grin beginning on his face. "That guy is one hard-headed son of a gun. The bullet was angled in such a way that it was deflected off his cranium. An eighth of an inch either way and he wouldn't be with us."

"Is he going to be all right?" Stacy asked.

"He's lost a lot of blood, but other than that, I think he's going to be fine. We ran all the appropriate tests for head wounds, including a CAT scan. He passed them all."

"Thank the good Lord for that," Arcenaux said.

"I'd like to keep him overnight for observation. He could use a good steak dinner and good night's rest. You can have him back tomorrow, Miss Stimmons."

"May I see him?" she asked.

"They'll be taking him up to his room in a few minutes. No reason why you can't be with him."

"Thank you so much for your help, Doctor."

"Thank you, Miss Stimmons. It's already spread over the hospital what you and Mr. Townsend did. As one who sees first hand the havoc drugs plays with lives, I am most grateful to both of you. It's a privilege to be of help." He shook Mitch's and Arcenaux's hand turned the corner and was gone.

"Hot dog. We can both get out of here tomorrow," Mitch said.

The door to the examining room opened and two nurses pushed Ryan's gurney down the hall. He was conscious and grinning that devilishly wicked grin at her. She took his hand in hers and walked beside the gurney. Mitch and Arcenaux followed.

Mitch laid his hand on Ryan's shoulder, "Wait'll I tell you what I have in mind. You're going to love it."

Arcenaux interrupted. "Well, if I get a move on ya'll, I can get an afternoon plane back to New Orleans. Wanted to make sure Ryan was all right." He shook Ryan and Mitch's hand and winked mischievously at Mitch.

"Miss Stimmons, if nothing's holding you down here, I'd be glad to escort you back," he said grinning from ear to ear.

"Oh, no you don't," Mitch said. "Ryan and I have plans for Miss Stimmons."

"*Chérie*, I wouldn't want to be in yo shoes for anything. See y'all back in New Orleans."

"Thanks for everything, Chief," Mitch said as Arcenaux closed the door behind himself.

Stacy stepped to Ryan's bed, bent, and kissed his bandage and then his lips. "Oh, Ryan, I was so scared. I thought you were dead. I realized at that moment, I was too. I don't ever want to take the chance of not being with you. Let's get married as soon as possible."

"Are you proposing to me, Lady?"

"Yes, yes, I guess I am."

Ryan glanced at Mitch. "Any reason why we can't hire a copter and catch up with the cruise ship?"

Stacy's eyes beamed with joy.

"That's just what I was thinking. I'll make the arrangements," Mitch said. "I need to make a call to Danielle. Don't suppose you two mind being alone for a little while, do you?"

Ryan had locked Stacy into his arms. They shared a kiss that made even Mitch blush. "Guess not," he said to himself as he quietly closed the door.

"Danielle, this is Mitch."

"Mitch, I've been so worried. Where are you?"

"Right now, I'm at Doctor's Hospital in Montego Bay."

"Are you okay?"

"Yeah, I'm fine. Ryan got creased, but he's going to be fine. They're going to let both of us out of here tomorrow. Danielle, I want to ask. . . ."

"What's wrong with you? You sound terrible."

"I just swallowed some salt water. I told you, I'm fine. Now don't interrupt. I have two important questions to ask you."

Danielle said, "Yes, Mitch."

"Yes? I haven't asked the questions, yet."

"I know, but we've lost too much time already. Whatever you want the answer is yes."

"Danielle, I love you. I even loved you when you wore those Shirley Temple curls and begged me to swing you higher. I've always loved you."

"I loved you too, Mitch, even then."

"Well, listen. That other question? You may not want to do this and whatever you decide is all right with me, but this is a great opportunity."

"What is it, Mitch?"

"Would you mind sharing your wedding day?"

"What do you mean?"

"This whole episode has brought Stacy to her senses. She and Ryan are getting married right away. They're going to get a copter, catch up with their cruise ship, and be married aboard."

"Oh, I'm so glad."

"I thought you might buy two wedding dresses, and get on a plane for Jamaica. I'll meet you at the airport. You and I can catch up with their cruise. We could have a double wedding aboard, and honeymoon in St. Barts.

"Oh, Mitch, that's a wonderful idea. I know Stacy would be glad to see the wedding dress but is this what they want?"

Mitch was dumbfounded. "I forgot to ask. But if it's not, we'll have our own wedding."

Danielle said, "Listen Mitch, if I get to Saks before

they close, I know they'll stay until I can get the dresses and things I need. I can get a plane out tomorrow morning."

"That sounds great, I'll call you back later tonight to make sure everything is working on your end. I love you, Danielle. One more thing. I'm afraid you'll have to wait until we get to St. Barts for a ring."

"What? No ring, no deal, Mr. McGalliard." Danielle laughed. "You know I'll be there, Sweetheart. See you then."

Mitch stopped at the cafeteria for a cup of coffee before returning to Ryan's room. He wanted to give Ryan and Stacy some time alone. After what they had been through, they had a lot to talk about. He sipped the coffee slowly. Suddenly, he remembered he'd just walked off from the wheelchair. He laughed to himself. Danielle could do that to a guy.

Mitch rapped on the door and pushed it open slowly.

"Come on in, Mitch," Stacy said.

Ryan looked up at Mitch, his brow wrinkled. "Mitch, tell us what happened to you out there."

"They met me at the plane. We got on a boat out on the peninsula. When we got out to sea. They relieved me of the money and dumped me in the drink. I thought I was a goner."

"How did you get back?" Stacy asked.

"I was in the water long enough to get my face

261

cooked pretty good. I heard a whirlybird bird, looked up, two guys jumped out, put me in a basket, hauled me up and there was Arcenaux. Jim Dandy to the rescue as always."

"How did he get involved?"

"I called him when I received the letter. He had a couple of men rig my jacket with a wire and homing device. The jacket got left on board when they threw me over. That's how they caught those thugs."

"Did they recover the money?"

"Yeah. I sent it back with Arcenaux. It's safer with him."

"Mitch, you know there's no way Stacy and I can ever thank you for what you did for us."

"Oh, yes there is. You can name the first boy after me."

"It's a deal," Ryan said. "Joshiah Mitchell Townsend." He put his hand out for Mitch to shake.

"Ryan, we've been through thick and thin since we were boys. A handshake won't do it." He bent over the bed. The two men hugged each other. Stacy smiled, her eyes glistening as she watched two friends who were more like brothers.

"Listen, both of you boys could use some rest. I'm going to locate a room for the night. You two get some sleep. I'll see you in the morning."

"Not until I get a steak as big as I am," Ryan said.

"Me too," Mitch added.

Stacy rolled her eyes and shook her head. "Little boys." She closed the door behind herself.

The next morning, Mitch saw Ryan and Stacy off on the helicopter. He bought a huge bouquet of tropical flowers and waited for Danielle's plane to land.

She looked fantastic. Her long auburn hair blew loosely in the breeze. Her pearl gray silk suit glistened like silver as she crossed the tarmac and went into Mitch's waiting arms.

"God, it's good to feel you," he said burying his face in her scented hair. "I have a helicopter waiting. We need to hurry."

"We must get my luggage. I'm afraid I've got several pieces."

"Somehow, I was certain you would," he teased.

Seagulls following the ship cried out, begging bites of bread from a group of children. The sun felt warm and comforting on Stacy's shoulders and bare legs. Ryan had stripped off his shirt to absorb the sun's warm rays. They enjoyed a glass of wine and a tray of tidbits while lounging on the deck and tried desperately to let their minds dismiss the perils of the preceding days.

"Ryan, can we renovate Dawn's Promise? It could be such a beautiful place."

"I was hoping you'd want to. That's been a dream

of mine for a long time. I'd like to do it for Aunt Sue."

Teasingly she added, "Yes, and any governor of Louisiana could use an estate with roots going back to year one."

He grinned. "Yeah, that too. Do you mind if I reach that far?"

"It's what you were made to do, Ryan. Uncle Josh taught you the values you possess for a reason. Don't let them go to waste. Louisiana needs you." She paused. "Can I have the painting of your mother and the horse?"

"No, but I'll share it with you."

"Well, you are learning to compromise, aren't you?"

"I'm trying. What do you want with the painting?"

"I want to paint the dining room the same peachy color as the apartment and hang the painting over the mantel so she can preside over the dinners we'll be giving to help get you elected. That's where she belongs."

"God Stacy, you're wonderful." He bent over to kiss her, almost tipping over the chaise lounge.

The whirring sound of a helicopter interrupted their conversation. A crowd gathered at the back of the ship. Ryan removed his sunglasses to get a better look at the commotion.

"Want to go see what's going on?" he asked.

"Why not? I'm going to take my wine with me."

One of the crew was in the process of opening the

door of the old military Huey. It had been converted to a helibus for carrying passengers and luggage between the islands. Mitch's head poked through the door sporting a wide smile. Ryan and Stacy stood there with their mouths open as they watched Danielle follow him.

"What are you two doing here?" Ryan asked.

"Well, I told you I had an idea," Mitch yelled over the noise of the copter. "I called Danielle and asked her to marry me. She said yes."

Danielle drawled in her most honey-lamb voice, "Came as a complete surprise." She laughed.

"Mitch, that's wonderful. I'm so happy for both of you," Stacy said. She hugged Danielle.

Ryan put forth his hand. "Congratulations, old man. You two deserve to be happy. You've waited long enough." He gave Danielle a hug and a kiss on the cheek.

"Thanks. I thought if you two agreed, we'd make it a double wedding," Mitch said.

Stacy threw her arms around Mitch's neck. "Mitch, what a wonderful idea. There's nothing I'd like better. You and Danielle are like family. Say yes, Ryan," Stacy pleaded.

"I think it's a great idea."

"Stacy, wait till you see what I've brought," Danielle said. She turned to see the crew-taking luggage off the helicopter.

"You can put Mrs. Parker's things in my cabin,"

Stacy said. "There's plenty of room."

"Looks like I'm bunking with you, Ryan," Mitch said.

"No way, I intend to do better than that," he said grinning at Stacy. Stacy blushed and turned back to Danielle.

"Come on. I have to show you some things I bought," Danielle said. The two women disappeared into the ship giggling like teenagers.

Stacy's eyes glistened when Danielle opened the boxes with the beautiful dresses in them. She placed her hands on her cheeks, disbelieving the cloud of perfection she saw.

"Oh, Danielle, I had already given up the idea of having a wedding dress. Just to have Ryan in one piece was all I really wanted. It's so beautiful I'm afraid it will melt if I touch it."

"The lace and beading is all hand done. I was a little pressed for time so I got them both alike. I hope you don't mind."

"Mind? I think it's perfect," Stacy said.

Danielle continued to unwrap shoes, hair ornaments, veils, and lacy undergarments. The box seemingly possessed no bottom.

"Have you and Ryan made the arrangements as to when the wedding will be held?" Danielle asked.

"Yes, it's scheduled for eight this evening. The whole ship is invited. Will that rush you too much?"

"You can't make it too soon for me. I've waited all

my life for this man," Danielle said.

The evening was warm and still. The moon played hopscotch over the gentle waves of the ocean. The deck of the ship had been converted to the Chelsea Flower Show. The band played softly *Come Saturday Morning.*

Stacy and Danielle emerged from the ship on the arms of smartly uniformed young officers and proceeded down a red carpet to the center of the deck. Attired in dress whites, members of the crew formed a corridor along the carpet. Ryan and Mitch waited at the end with the captain.

As Stacy gazed at Ryan in his black tuxedo and ruffled shirt, the memory of Lafitte standing on a pirate ship, dressed in black from head to toe with a white ruffled shirt, flashed across her mind. The evening breeze tousled his raven hair. His black eyes gleamed at the sight of her and the inevitable crooked grin didn't frighten but excited her. Just as before, she thought him the most handsome man she had ever seen.

The *Wedding March* began. Ryan's dark eyes locked onto Stacy's and he never let them stray the entire procession. She reached his side and he bent to whisper, "Stacy, you're the most beautiful bride I have ever seen. You are my treasure."

THE END